SHADOW GUARDIAN
AND THE THREE BEARS

SHADOW GUARDIAN SERIES

SHADOW GUARDIAN
AND THE THREE BEARS

ROBERT J. LEWIS

4 Horsemen
Publications, Inc.

4 Horsemen
Publications, Inc.

4 Horsemen Publications, Inc.
1497 Main St. Suite 169
Dunedin, FL 34698
4horsemenpublications.com
info@4horsemenpublications.com

Cover and Typeset by S. Wilder
Editor Kristine Cotter

Library of Congress Control Number: 2022943658

Print ISBN: 979-8-8232-0031-8
Hardcover ISBN: 979-8-8232-0032-5
Ebook ISBN: 979-8-8232-0030-1
Audio ISBN: 979-8-8232-0018-9

Of course, this is dedicated to my parents, may they rest in peace. To Bonita, my little diva. To all of my family and friends who have encouraged me. Thank you.

UI

TABLE OF CONTENTS

PROLOGUE

HIDING IN THE ALLEY ACROSS FROM THE BAR
where Juan Carlos worked, Diego watched the patrons
coming and going. He still had a few weeks before he'd be old
enough to enter legally. He wasn't trying to get in, though. If
he wanted to, he could use the employee entrance Juan Carlos
sometimes let him use to watch the shows.

Diego wasn't there to see a show. He was there to keep watch,
to stand guard. In the past month, someone had attacked ten
people leaving the bar, raping, beating, and violating them
with random objects. Two hadn't survived. They didn't expect
three to ever walk again. All who survived would need years
of extensive therapy. Diego would be damned if he'd let that
happen to Juan Carlos, or anyone else for that matter.

The victims had all left the bar alone, choosing to walk the
dangerous streets instead of spending a couple of bucks on a
ride. The people he saw came and went in groups of three or
more. These people had obviously learned, arming themselves

with numbers and common sense since the police weren't doing anything about it.

The police called the incidents isolated. The politicians were blaming the victims for frequenting a sinful establishment. That's why Diego was there. It was what Juan Carlos had taught him. To look out for your community. To do what you can for the community. This was what Diego felt he could do for his community.

Diego stood, poised to take action. *I am a panther—a guardian in the shadows, ready to protect and defend.* Diego scanned the front of the bar. *I have nothing to fear except Juan Carlos finding out I'm here.* Shifting his feet, Diego yawned. *Freddy had better not rat me out.*

A hand on Diego's shoulder caused him to let out a high-pitched screech. He turned, fist raised, to attack his would-be assailant. His body was tense and ready to strike. He was ready for anything, anything except the disapproving glare of Juan Carlos. Slumping his shoulders, Diego lowered his hands and prepared for the inevitable scolding.

Juan Carlos crossed his arms, the sleeves of his flowing robe hanging down his body. The clack of his high-heeled boot and the cement was the only thing Diego heard. He knew Juan Carlos was waiting for him to explain himself, to justify why he was out here.

"Well?" Juan Carlos asked when the silence between them dragged out too long. "I have a show in twenty minutes. Start explaining."

Diego shuffled his feet but kept his eyes up, meeting Juan Carlos's. He squared his shoulders and said in a tone that was defiant yet respectful, "I'm protecting my community. I'm making sure no one gets attacked."

Juan Carlos mulled over the words. He wanted to reprimand Diego, but couldn't. "We have it covered. We have a network of volunteers making sure everyone comes and goes from the bar safely." Juan Carlos unfolded his arms, the sleeves billowing out. "Where is Federico?"

Diego rolled his eyes. "He got that weird look in his eyes and started drawing again. I told him I was leaving, but I don't think he heard me."

Concern etched in Juan Carlos's voice. "You know you're not supposed to leave him alone. You're supposed to look out for each other."

Diego kicked the ground. "He never wants to do anything fun, like video games or watch television. All he does is draw or some artsy thing. Plus, he's always sniffing me. That's weird."

"You know he's photosensitive. That's why Esmerelda left him with you." Diego felt a twinge of guilt at Juan Carlos's soft reprimand. "And I'll talk to Esmerelda about the sniffing."

Diego's lips curled into a slight smile before flattening out again. "Okay, no more sneaking out, but I'm going to learn to fight."

Diego found himself wrapped in Juan Carlos's flowing robe. "Aye, niño mio. Will you be my little boy one more night? You can grow up tomorrow."

Diego held onto Juan Carlos. "You can't protect me forever."

Running his hand over the back of Diego's head, Juan Carlos said, "I know, but I can try." Juan Carlos kissed the top of Diego's head. "I'll talk to Esmerelda about having Federico train you, but you should use that big brain of yours instead of your fists."

The two held onto each other a moment longer. Wiping a tear away as he pulled away, Diego asked, "Can't I use both?"

Juan Carlos took Diego's hand. "As long as you use them to make our community better. Now, let's get you home."

Crossing the street, they stopped in front of the bar. Juan Carlos took Diego by the shoulders so he could look the young man in the eyes. "Be my little boy until morning, okay?" Juan Carlos kissed Diego on the cheek. "Gato, make sure he gets home safe."

Diego looked at the slender, muscular Latinx man with colorful tattoos decorating the length of both arms who placed a hand on his shoulder. "As if my life depended upon it."

"Good, because it does." Juan Carlos gave Gato a look that told him he meant business.

"You just make sure to put in that good word with Esmerelda for me." Gato countered.

Juan Carlos waved his hand flippantly in the air, his shiny, red nails catching the bar light. "I'll do what I can. You need to show her you can be the man she needs you to be."

Gato straightened, standing proudly and boldly. "You know I can be."

"Yes. Yes, you can be. Unfortunately, right now, you're not." Juan Carlos's words were razor sharp. "Now get my boy home. Don't forget you're escorting our futures home."

"Come on, Rico, let's get this special care package home." A stocky, broad-shouldered man appeared beside Gato. "Apparently, he's our future."

CHAPTER 1

ALEX WALKED HOME FROM THE BAR ALONE. He knew he shouldn't be walking alone at night, but the spring air was cool, and he didn't have enough money for a ride home. The bar was only a few blocks from his apartment, and unfortunately, no one was interested in going home with him, not even on a slow Wednesday karaoke night.

Alex was two blocks from his place when he heard the footsteps behind him. He felt the fear in the pit of his stomach. He didn't run, but he picked up his pace. Whoever it was behind him matched his pace. He was ready to run when the footsteps stopped and there was the sound of a door opening and closing.

You're overreacting. Just get your ass home and get to bed. You have to work tomorrow, he berated himself. Alex kept on, jumping at every sound. *Why did you have to go out tonight? To meet someone? No one is ever interested in you.*

Alex was mentally berating himself when someone yanked him into the darkness of an alleyway. He landed hard on the filthy pavement; the breath knocked from his body. He felt himself get lifted into the air, then he crashed against the brick wall. Pain shot through his body. His vision blurred and was littered with stars.

"Look what we have here. Looks like we're going to have a little fun tonight," a gruff voice snarled.

"Can I have him first?" a greasy voice asked off to the side. Alex blinked, trying to clear his vision. "I like it when they have a little fight left in them. I like to hear them scream."

Alex could barely make out the face of the bloated man that pinned him to the wall. He could smell the stench of stale cigarettes and cheap beer on his breath. "He'll still scream." The reality of the situation was sinking in for Alex. "If you're rough enough."

"Come on. The last one was dead when I got him," Greasy whined.

Alex panicked. He struggled in vain against the man. "Please, don't do this. Please, just let me go." The men laughed, amused by Alex's fear-driven pleas. "I'll give you anything you want. Please don't hurt me."

The gruff man laughed. "What we want is to hurt you. And my friend here wants to know what you feel like." Alex felt himself flying in the air, then jolting pain when he crashed into a dumpster. "Go on. You want him first. Take him. Make it quick."

Alex struggled to get up. "Please, no." He screamed when he felt the first kick into his ribs. He curled into a ball. Tears streamed down his cheeks. Greasy laughed above him as he kept kicking Alex. "Please, stop."

Alex felt hands on him, clawing at his clothes. "Come on, let's get you naked. Doesn't matter how loud you scream. They're used to it by now, and nobody cares." Alex kicked and swung his arms wildly about, trying to fend the man off. "Yeah, he's got some fight in him."

"Stop!" Alex screamed in a choked sob. He closed his eyes, not wanting to see the man that was about to violate him. "Please, don't do this!" Alex kept kicking and flailing at the greasy man, but it only seemed to amuse him. "Stop! Stop! Please, stop!"

Alex swung his arms and kicked madly, but he landed no blows. It took him a moment to realize the hands that had been clawing at him were gone. He opened his tear-soaked eyes. Alex couldn't believe what he was seeing. He had to be hallucinating. He saw the two men struggling with some sort of creature. No. A man.

Alex heard the crunch of bone when his savior's fist collided with the gruff man's jaw. The stranger picked up the greasy man and slung him down the alley past Alex. Alex watched the greasy man struggle to get up, then run away into the darkness. Alex turned his attention back to the entrance of the alley to see the gruff man on the ground, motionless, his savior standing over him.

The shadowy figure moved toward Alex. Alex watched in disbelief as the massive man came closer, his features distorted by the darkness. Alex knew it was him. It had to be him. There was no one else it could be. Alex couldn't believe he was being saved by him, of all people. The one everyone talked about in hush whispers.

"Shadow Guardian. It's really you," Alex croaked out, a slight twinge of awe in his voice.

Shadow Guardian crouched down beside Alex. "You need medical attention." Shadow Guardian reached out and checked Alex's ribs. Alex tried to look into the faceless black mask that swirled with grey smoke. "I'll get you to a hospital. Can you stand?"

Alex winced when he tried to get up. "I'm okay. I can't afford a hospital." Shadow Guardian carefully lifted him up.

"Thank you." Alex tried to stand on his own, but he stumbled. He found strong arms holding up his bruised body. "Thank you again."

"You really should get checked out by a doctor," Shadow Guardian admonished. "Let me take you to a hospital."

"I'm fine. I just need to get home. I was almost there when those guys grabbed me," Alex argued. He tried to push away from Shadow Guardian, but he refused to let Alex go. "Look, I'm just a little bruised. I'll be okay after a good night's sleep."

"I'll take you home then," Shadow Guardian relented. "There's no way you can make it on your own."

"Fine. I'm just two more blocks down." Alex tried, and failed, not to smile. He didn't want to argue. This was Shadow Guardian, Morgan City's mysterious protector. The man he'd jerked off to on more than one occasion. "Thank you, again."

Shadow Guardian slipped an arm around Alex. "Let's get you home. Lean on me. I got you." Alex put his arm around Shadow Guardian, pleasantly surprised that the hardness under his touch was Shadow Guardian, not armor or padding. If he moved his hand just a little, he'd touch that glorious ass. "Are you ready?"

Alex gripped Shadow Guardian tighter, praying he couldn't read minds. He took a stumbling step forward. "Yes. This way." Alex leaned against Shadow Guardian as they walked, wondering what he felt like under that suit. They stepped over the passed-out brute. "You should be more careful."

Alex thought he heard a hint of concern in Shadow Guardian's voice but knew he was reading too much into it. "I normally am. I don't usually go out on Wednesday nights. I, uh, figured I'd change it up a bit."

"You shouldn't have been walking home alone. You should have walked home with someone or gotten a ride," Shadow Guardian chided.

Alex didn't want to explain to him that he didn't have anyone to walk home with or that he couldn't afford a ride home. It was embarrassing enough that he had to be rescued; he didn't want to have to explain that he had spent the evening in a bar being ignored and couldn't afford a ride. "I know. I won't be going out anytime soon, anyway. Not like this."

They didn't speak again until they were in front of Alex's rundown building. "This is me. Thank you again for rescuing me and for helping me home," Alex said with a twinge of embarrassment in his voice. Alex tried to pull away, but Shadow Guardian did not let go. "Um, I can take it from here."

"What floor are you on?" He waited a moment for Alex to answer before asking again. "What floor are you on?"

"Four. The top floor." Alex sucked on the inside of his cheek before adding, "No, there's no working elevator." Shadow Guardian scooped Alex up into his arms. "Hey, wait, what are you doing? Put me down. What the hell, man?"

Shadow Guardian turned his head to look at Alex. He could feel Shadow Guardian's eyes on him through the faceless mask. "You couldn't walk down the street without help. How do you think you're going to fare with stairs?" Alex put his arm around Shadow Guardian's neck. "That's what I thought."

Shadow Guardian maneuvered them through the door and up the stairs. Alex tried to act like he hated every minute of it, but the reality was that he loved every moment of it. Truthfully, he didn't want it to end. He cursed every step that brought them closer to his apartment. Aside from the incident in the alley, this was his first human contact in he didn't know how long.

Alex tried to hide the disappointment when they arrived at his apartment. "This is me. You can put me down now. I got it from here."

"Keys," Shadow Guardian said simply.

Alex groaned, making a show of his false displeasure as he fumbled for the keys to his apartment. He made a show of pulling them out of his front pocket and said, "Fine. Here. How are you going to—" Shadow Guardian dropped to one knee, so Alex was able to reach the knob. "Okay, that answers that question."

Alex opened the door, wishing he had cleaned up or something for his unexpected guest. Instead of being set down, as Alex had expected, Shadow Guardian stood and carried Alex into his apartment. "We should get your cuts cleaned up, so they don't get infected." Shadow Guardian laid Alex on his broken couch. "Where's your first aid kit?"

"I might have a band-aid in my medicine cabinet," Alex answered sheepishly. Alex could tell by the cock of Shadow Guardian's head that he was looking at him in disbelief. "What? It's not like I was expecting to be attacked by two guys who wanted to murder and rape me tonight."

Alex watched Shadow Guardian walk into his kitchen. "I haven't gone grocery shopping if you're looking for something to eat," Alex called out when he saw Shadow Guardian going through his cabinets. "What are you looking for?" Alex watched Shadow Guardian find a dish towel and a small bowl that he filled with water.

Shadow Guardian returned to Alex's side. He crouched down, dipped the towel in water, and began cleaning the cut on Alex's forehead. "Ouch." Alex flinched. "Why are you doing this?"

Shadow Guardian dipped the cloth in water and returned to cleaning Alex's wounds. "Because no one else in the city will. The police do nothing around here unless they get paid."

"I mean this. Cleaning me up."

Shadow Guardian wiped the last of the blood from Alex's face. "Because no one else in this city will, and you won't go to a hospital." Shadow Guardian stood. Taking the cloth and bowl to the kitchen, he asked, "Will you be okay alone?"

Shadow Guardian was now standing over him. Alex was momentarily mesmerized by the smoky gray curls that moved around Shadow Guardian's suit. "Yeah, uh, yeah. I'll be fine." Alex winced as he sat up. "I have to get to bed. I have to work in the morning."

"Take care of yourself." Alex watched Shadow Guardian walk to the door. Shadow Guardian paused after opening the door. Turning his head, he said, "I'll be checking up on you." Then he was gone, out the door and out of Alex's life.

CHAPTER 2

From the comfort of the backseat of his car, Diego watched the front of the building. People filled the sidewalks, coming and going, but Diego was watching for one particular individual. One that had unexpectedly caught his interest. One that he needed to know more about.

Diego's heart jumped when he spotted his prey coming out of the building in desperate need of attention. He hid the bruises on his honey brown skin under a frayed white dress shirt and faded black pants. He carried a worn messenger bag draped across his chest. A cut above his right eye was scabbed over. Diego could tell he was in pain by the way he winced slightly as he walked.

Something intrigued and worried Diego about this man. "Meet me at the office," Diego said to Juan Carlos before slipping out of the car. He maneuvered through the people rushing on the sidewalk to start their days while keeping one eye on his query doing the same across the street.

When the man stopped across the street, so did Diego. The man stood at the entrance of a boarded-up storefront. A teen shyly came out of the shadows. To the teen's dismay, the man rustled the teen's hair. The man pulled out a brown paper bag from his messenger bag. Diego expected the teen to pull out drugs when he reached into the bag but was pleasantly surprised when it was a sandwich.

Diego could see the teen was complaining about the sandwich. The teen shoved the sandwich into the bag and gave the man a hug. The man messed up the teen's hair again before he was off, leaving the teen to fade back into the shadows. Diego followed, pondering the man's oddly sweet actions.

Diego watched him stop again. This time in front of a slumped-over homeless man, passed out and clinging to a bottle of booze. He took the empty bottle from the man's hand, tossed it in the trash, then pulled another brown bag from his bag and set it in front of the man. Then he turned his attention to the two empty bowls beside the man.

From his bag, he pulled out a bottle of water and poured it into one of the bowls, then pulled out a small bag of dog food that he dumped it into the other. A small dog perked up from beside the man. The man scratched the tiny yipping happy dog behind the ears before it turned its attention to the now full bowls.

The man continued on, helping an elderly woman get her cart up the stairs to the train platform, then helping her onto the train and then off the train two stops later. At his stop, he paused to toss some coins into the open guitar case of a street performer before heading on into work.

Diego paused, contemplating what he had just observed. The man did not make sense. No one was this nice. He'd have to see what Juan Carlos found on this man. He had been working at his job for the past three years as an entry-level temp worker with no raise or offer to be hired on permanently. That was odd. Especially since it was Diego's company, and they had a policy of hiring temps or letting them go after six months.

Diego saw his car parked, waiting for him. He could have strolled into the building in his jeans and tee shirt, but he didn't want to get an earful from Juan Carlos on the importance of dressing the part of a powerful CEO of a Fortune 500 company. Sometimes he wished he was still a struggling nobody trying to make it.

As soon as Diego slipped into the car, it pulled out into traffic. Diego quickly changed behind the tinted windows. "Make sure your tie is straight," Juan Carlos said from behind the wheel. "Don't forget the kerchief or the diamond tie tack. They make the outfit."

"I won't, papi," Diego teased.

"What did I tell you about calling me that?" Juan Carlos snipped back, carefully turning the corner to circle the block.

"Sí, mamacita," Diego prodded, slipping on his shoes. "I want you to do a full background check on him."

"Your mouth is going to get you in trouble someday." Juan Carlos pulled into the private underground garage. "Did you see something that raised your suspicions?"

Diego straightened his tie. "No, quite the opposite. He seems sweet and nice. We need to find out why he hasn't been hired or gotten a raise in the last three years. That's unusual. You know our policy on temps."

Juan Carlos pulled into the parking spot. "That is unusual. I wonder if there are any others that have slipped through the cracks."

Diego stepped out of the car. "I think maybe it's time you did an audit of the company. And don't forget to do another background check on Alex. I wonder if what happened last night was a setup."

Juan Carlos snickered, adjusting Diego's coat. "You think he's a honey trap? Trust me, baby, he's no honey trap." Juan Carlos brushed Diego's coat. "You do realize that sometimes people are sweet and nice."

"Not where we come from." Diego rolled his neck, then turned and walked to the private elevator. "If it weren't for you, I'd probably still be running the streets."

"See, I was sweet and nice." Juan Carlos fell in step with Diego.

Diego laughed, pressing the button for the elevator. "You were bitter and mean. The first time I met you, you smacked me upside my head and told me my beauty would fade, but my stupidity would last forever."

"I caught you trying to spray paint 'fuck the police' on my house." They stepped into the elevator. "My house," Juan Carlos emphasized, "and you misspelled both fuck and police. I was honestly surprised you spelled 'the' correctly."

Diego laughed. "Then you made me go inside and write 'Fuck the police' a hundred times in my best handwriting. You heard my stomach growl, so you made me lunch."

"Feed a stray cat," Juan Carlos teased. "You came back the next day and scrubbed the wall."

Diego glanced over at Juan Carlos. "You watched me for an hour before you came out with a bucket of paint and helped me paint over it. Then you took me inside and made me lunch."

Juan Carlos's lips curled slightly. "Then I found out you weren't going to school, and I threatened to beat your ass. I made you come over every day after school to do your homework."

Diego put an arm around Juan Carlos and pulled him into a side hug. "You were more of a mother and father than my own were. You were the only one who ever believed in me. That encouraged me."

Juan Carlos put an arm around Diego. "Stop that. Your parents did the best they knew how. I just knew more."

"I know." Diego let go. "They gave me life. You taught me to live and dream." The elevator opened. Diego turned, allowing Juan Carlos to inspect him. "Thank you. Find out more about this Alex. I have work to do."

Juan Carlos stepped back into the elevator. "Right away. Remember, you also need to review Dr. Wyatt's progress sometime today."

Diego gave a half smile. "I'll make it a priority. You don't like him or his work, do you?"

Juan Carlos pressed the button in the elevator. "No," he said as the doors shut.

CHAPTER 3

A LEX SAT RIGID IN THE SEAT IN JUAN Carlos's office. It had been ten minutes since he entered the office and was told to sit down. Juan Carlos continued typing away on his computer as if Alex wasn't even there. He would have said something, but who was he to interrupt one of the co-founders of the company?

Juan Carlos suddenly stopped what he was doing, then turned his attention to Alex, his face stern yet fatherly. "You don't like rocking the boat or making waves, do you?"

"No, sir," Alex croaked out. "I'm very happy here," he added quickly.

Juan Carlos studied a folder on his desk. "You must really love it here. You've been a temp here for the last three years. You know we have a hire or fire policy for temps after six months." Alex's stomach twisted in knots. "You have a computer science and programming degree—top of your class. One of your professors said you taught him something new.

That makes me wonder: why have you been doing data entry for the past three years?"

"I, uh, was grateful to have a job here. It's good work," Alex answered honestly.

"Your grandmother raised you. When she passed away last year, we didn't pay you for the week of work that you missed." Juan Carlos's voice grew somber. "I'm sorry for your loss." Alex tried not to tear up. "I'm also sorry that we cannot continue to employ you as a temp in data entry."

Alex panicked, nearly jumping out of his chair to plead his case. "Please, no. I need this job. I have a lot of debt."

Juan Carlos cleared his throat. "I am, however, going to offer you a position in our Special Projects department." Alex couldn't believe what he was hearing. "It comes with a significant raise and benefits. If you accept the position." Alex was almost in tears; he was so happy. "You'll also be receiving a check for back pay for all your missed raises, the week you had to take off work, and the vacation time you should have been given."

Alex wiped away a stray tear from his cheek. "Oh, my God. Thank you. I'll take the job, yes." For once in his life, something was going right for him. "Thank you. Thank you. Thank you."

Juan Carlos leaned forward, staring intently at Alex. "Do you really want to thank me? Take a bit of advice from me and put it to good use." Alex leaned forward, eager for whatever sage wisdom Juan Carlos was willing to bestow upon him. "When you toss a pebble into the water, it barely makes a splash. It's almost unnoticeable. Toss a boulder into the water, and it makes a big splash that everyone notices."

Alex wasn't sure what Juan Carlos was talking about until he added the rest. "You did data entry for three years. You didn't get a raise for three years. Didn't get any vacation time.

Then in here, you let me type away at my computer while you waited." Juan Carlos's tone grew fatherly. "Don't be a pebble. Be a boulder. Make a big splash. Don't be afraid to make big waves. Make everyone notice."

Alex nodded. "Yes, sir. I'm not sure I know how, but I will. I promise."

"I'll teach you. I'm in charge of Special Projects." Juan Carlos leaned back in his chair, flashing his smile at Alex. "I expect great things from you."

Alex jumped up and reached out his hand to Juan Carlos. "I won't let you down. Thank you again, sir. You won't be disappointed. I promise."

Juan Carlos stood and took Alex's hand. "You're welcome. Now go. My assistant, Dion, will go over the details. I'm just sorry it took us this long to correct this error." Juan Carlos felt a twinge of satisfaction as he watched the young man leave. He took a moment to compose himself before sitting down and calling Diego.

"What happened? How did it go?" Diego asked, bluntly and to the point.

"Manners," Juan Carlos scolded.

"I'm sorry." Juan Carlos could hear the impishness in Diego's tone. "How are you, mamacita?"

"I'm well, except for this pain in my ass. I named it Diego," Juan Carlos shot back before growing serious. "It's done. He's no longer a temp in data entry."

"Oh." Juan Carlos heard the disappointment in Diego's voice. "I'm sorry to hear that. Did you find out anything else?"

"Clean as the floors I used to scrub to put you through college," Juan Carlos answered.

"That dirty?"

"You do not bad mouth my cleaning. Bendejo," Juan Carlos growled through the phone.

Diego laughed. "Lo siento, mamacita. I really wish it had turned out better. We'll talk after I visit Dr. Wyatt's lab. Send me what you found on him. Maybe you missed something."

"I missed nothing," Juan Carlos huffed. "Sent."

CHAPTER 4

D IEGO TRIED NOT TO LET THE NEWS OF ALEX
being let go bother him. He had hoped that Juan Carlos
would see something in the young man like he had seen in
Diego. He had reviewed everything Juan Carlos sent up that
he had gathered on Alex. There was nothing that he saw that
sent up red flags. Sure, he lacked ambition. From what he
saw this morning, he had a lot of heart. That had to count for
something.

Diego pushed that away for now. He had to check in on Dr.
Wyatt and his project. It wasn't one Diego was entirely comfortable with. Apparently, there was a societal need for it, or so
Dr. Wyatt claimed. The idea was an alternative to medical pro-
cedures for weight loss, but Dr. Wyatt had grander designs. He
wanted it to be a revolutionary over-the-counter medication.

Diego wasn't comfortable with that. He believed the medication should be a last resort after proper diet and exercise.
That's how Diego did it. He was a chubby kid and struggled
with his weight during his teen years. Juan Carlos taught him

the virtues of loving himself, healthy eating, and proper exercise that changed his body.

Diego knew others weren't as fortunate as he was. He wanted to help them too, but some miracle pill wasn't the answer for everyone. It shouldn't be. Add that to the fact that they didn't know the short-term or long-term effects of the drug, and this pill could be the next big thing if it worked safely or the next big disaster if it didn't.

"Dr. Wyatt, how are you today?" Diego hated these forced pleasantries with Dr. Wyatt, but that was part of his job in dealing with men like Dr. Wyatt.

Dr. Wyatt looked up from his tablet screen. He pushed his glasses back up the bridge of his nose. A forced smile crept through Dr. Wyatt's reddish brown unkempt beard. Diego knew the man did not like to be bothered when he was working, or at all, for that matter. Dr. Wyatt had to understand that's not how things were done in the corporate world.

"I'm fine. Thank you for asking. Yourself?" The annoyance was evident in Dr. Wyatt's false pleasantry.

"Jimmy. Timmy." Diego nodded to Dr. Wyatt's research assistants, wondering how they lasted so long working for this intolerable man. "I've come to get a progress report. See how things are going with your project." Diego stepped farther into the lab, careful not to touch anything. He knew how it annoyed Dr. Wyatt to have his things touched.

Dr. Wyatt locked his tablet and pushed it aside. The contempt in his eyes for Diego was quite evident. "We're almost ready to submit permission for human testing." Dr. Wyatt did not move, making Diego come to him. "The simulations so far have been extremely promising."

Diego didn't trust Dr. Wyatt's simulations. He had lied about results before, fudged information, and then blamed it on his assistants incorrectly recording data when caught.

"Good. Good." Diego stayed on the other side of Dr. Wyatt's research table. "I'd like to see them, if you don't mind."

Dr. Wyatt let out a sound of annoyance. "Timmy." The gangly research assistant came to life, wordlessly bringing over a tablet to Diego. Timmy swiped the screen open, tapped the screen a few times, then handed the tablet to Diego before rushing away from him. "As you see, the medication acts like a reprogrammer, telling the body to stop storing fat and build muscle."

"It would be a godsend for people like Jimmy over there, to become fit and trim." Diego glanced at the larger man before turning his attention to the tablet. It looked pretty. He didn't have any other words for it. That made Diego suspicious. "It also has the effect of helping those struggling to put on weight by helping them build muscle." Dr. Wyatt motioned over to his other assistant. "Jimmy." The larger man struggled to get off his stool, then slowly made his way over to Diego. "Any time now, Jimmy."

Diego felt bad for the men. He'd have Juan Carlos talk to Dr. Wyatt about how he treated his assistants. He watched Jimmy tap away at the screen as Timmy had. "Here, sir," Jimmy said sheepishly, handing over the tablet. He looked at Diego for a brief moment, then lumbered back to his stool.

Diego caught Dr. Wyatt scowling at Jimmy. "As you can see, it tells the body to build muscle, so someone like Timmy over there," Diego looked over at the quiet man who quickly looked down at his work, "would turn from a scrawny tooth-pick to a gym god in a matter of days."

"These all look very promising. Send your data over. I'll have Juan Carlos run his own simulations, and if his results confirm yours, we'll start the paperwork for limited human trials." Diego sat the tablet down.

Dr. Wyatt closed his eyes. "Why must we go through this?" Opening his eyes, he glared at Diego with his cold blue eyes. "I've shown you the simulations. The drug works. Why can't we just get on with it? The sooner this goes to trial, the sooner we can have it out for the public. Why are you trying to impede my success in this?" Diego heard the restrained anger in Dr. Wyatt's voice.

Diego centered himself before answering. "Dr. Wyatt, you know this is the way things are done. You do your simulations. Then we do ours." He saw Dr. Wyatt grinding his teeth, trying to restrain himself. "If ours matches yours, then we apply for trials. That's how it works. That's how it always has worked, and that's how it's going to work."

"Fine," Dr. Wyatt said through clenched teeth. "I will have Jimmy and Timmy send up all the pertinent data."

"All the data. And I mean all the data." Diego emphasized every word.

Dr. Wyatt gave a slight nod to Diego. "All the data. If that is all, I'd like to get back to work."

Diego gave him a toothy smile. "Thank you. I look forward to reviewing the results. I'll let you get back to your work. Gentlemen." He nodded to each man. "I'm looking forward to celebrating your success." Diego walked out of the lab, not feeling any better about the project than he had before entering.

CHAPTER 5

A LEX HADN'T STOPPED SMILING SINCE leaving Juan Carlos's office. His assistant, Dion, a sweet young lady with a shaved head, had shown him where he would be working from now on. It was a huge office with a fantastic view of the city. It had all of the latest computers and software. He spent the rest of the day just playing and getting to know the systems. Before he knew it, Dion tapped on his door, reminding him that it was time to go home.

He still felt pain from the night before when he walked, but it had dulled. It took him a few extra minutes to climb the stairs to his apartment, but he didn't mind. Things were looking up for him for a change. The check for his back pay was already pending in his account. It would go a long way to paying off his debt.

He had been tempted to splurge on a celebratory dinner, but he couldn't do that. He needed every cent to pay off his debt. He'd stick to his peanut butter sandwiches for now. Even with his increase in pay, he still had years of debt to pay off, and he couldn't live peacefully until it was all gone.

He stepped into his apartment, feeling hopeful about the future for the first time in a long while. He paused two steps in. On his kitchen counter sat two brown bags and a plate covered in plastic wrap. He double-checked the door number, then looked back at the food. He rubbed his eyes, making sure he wasn't seeing things.

Closing the door, he went over to the food. He saw there was also a small bag of kibble and a bottle of water. "What the Hell?" He cocked an eyebrow. "Hello? Is there someone here?" He looked about his tiny apartment, finding nothing and no one. "Strange."

When he went back to the kitchen, he noticed the note stuck to the refrigerator. He pulled the note off.

I saw you needed to go grocery shopping, so I did it for you. Stop going out alone at night. Be safe.

SG.

Alex found his fridge stocked full when he opened it, the same with the cabinets and freezer when he checked them.

Alex wasn't sure if he should find it disturbing or touching that Shadow Guardian broke into his place, cooked him dinner, and left him a kitchen full of food. He decided to be touched. His grandmother was the only one he ever remembered cooking for him. What did disturb Alex were the two lunches and kibble that he had also been given.

"If you're watching or listening, it's kind of creepy!" Alex unwrapped the plate. His stomach growled at the delicious smell. "Thank you, too. It smells great!"

Alex grabbed something to drink and sat down on his broken sofa to eat. He said a silent prayer before cutting into the still warm meat. He allowed himself the small fantasy that he was sharing this meal with Shadow Guardian. He knew it was silly, but it made him happy. He figured he deserved a little bit of happiness.

After finishing his dinner, he washed his plate, took a shower, and slipped into a comfy pair of sleep pants and an old tee. He opened his bedroom window, letting in the fresh night air, then went back to the couch to relax with some television. It was the one luxury he afforded himself, though, after today, he could afford more.

He flipped through the channels, the lack of sleep from the night before catching up with him. After the third yawn, he sat up and decided to go to bed. That way, he could get to work early and play with all those new fancy toys. Suddenly, a shadow appeared above him. Not a shadow, but Shadow Guardian.

Alex jumped up, clutching his chest, his heart pounding. "What the fuck! How did you get in here?"

"Through your bedroom window." Shadow Guardian said like it was a completely obvious and acceptable answer. "You shouldn't leave your windows open. This isn't a good neighborhood."

"I live on the fourth floor of a building, and there isn't a fire escape. I think it's safe to leave my bedroom window open." Alex shot back.

"I got in," Shadow Guardian countered as if it were a perfectly reasonable argument. "You should also get better locks. It didn't take me two minutes to pick the locks."

"Who worries about...? No." Alex closed his eyes and laughed. He was arguing with Shadow Guardian. He smiled at how absurd this argument was. "I'll close my windows and get new locks. Thank you for dinner and the food."

"You're welcome. I saw you needed to go grocery shopping and weren't in any condition to do it yourself." Alex thought he saw the smoke swirling around Shadow Guardian's mouth curl into a smile. "Did you go see a doctor?"

"You know I didn't. You were watching me," Alex accused. "Thank you for making the meals for Pat, Benny, and Lily."

"I figured you could use the rest. How are you feeling?" Alex thought he heard a slight hint of bashfulness in Shadow Guardian's voice.

"I'm still a little sore," Alex confessed. "I won't be going dancing anytime soon. Not that I went dancing anyways."

"What do you do for fun?" The question threw Alex off. "You can't just work and feed random people on the street."

Alex shrugged. "I work on computers and my programming in my spare time. People around here come to me to fix their computers, tablets, and smartphones. I know other people wouldn't find it fun, but I do."

"Do you make a lot of money doing it?"

Alex laughed. "Money? No one around here has the money to fix their electronics. I do it for fun. I mean, they pay for any parts I need, but I don't charge them. It's like a good deed, you know?"

"Interesting. You know you could make some money doing it. A side hustle." There was a tone of suspicion in Shadow Guardian's voice.

"Not everything is about money."

"True." Shadow Guardian contemplated for a moment. "I should get back on patrol."

Alex stood, trying to see something in Shadow Guardian's faceless features. "I'll see you out. Thank you for stopping by."

"No problem." Shadow Guardian fidgeted a minute, then turned and headed toward Alex's bedroom. "Remember to change your locks and shut your window."

"Wait, where are you going?" Alex laughed. "Of course, you're leaving through the window." Alex followed. He stood awkwardly in his bedroom, watching Shadow Guardian climb out of his window. "You know, if you'd like to stop by again, I wouldn't mind."

"I'll be around." Shadow Guardian hung outside the window sill. "I'll be watching."

"I hope so," Alex said as Shadow Guardian disappeared. He closed the window, looking out to see if he could catch another glimpse of Shadow Guardian. "I really hope so."

CHAPTER 6

"WHAT'S WRONG?" JUAN CARLOS ASKED, walking into Diego's office. He found Diego staring absentmindedly out over the city. "And don't give me that nothing bullshit you've been telling me all day."

"There's nothing wrong. I'm fine," Diego answered, not turning around.

"At least give me the courtesy of turning and looking me in the face when you lie to me. Anyways, when you're done being fine, I need you to come see the simulations our new head programmer ran." Juan Carlos had a twinge of annoyance in his voice.

Diego turned around with a cocked eyebrow. "New head programmer? When did we get a new programmer, let alone a head programmer? And how did he run the simulations so quickly?"

Juan Carlos pretended to examine his nails. "Yesterday, and if you bring your sullen ass to the 'Special Projects' room, you'll meet the genius I hired."

Diego came around the desk. "I am not sullen. Fine, I am, but did you have to let Alex go from data entry?"

Juan Carlos headed to the private elevator. "Yes. Did you have to fill his kitchen with food and climb in his window last night?"

"I wanted to make sure he was okay after you let him go from his job at data entry. So, I wanted to make sure he had something to eat." Diego stepped into the elevator with Juan Carlos.

"Remember who you are talking to. Isn't he a little young for you?" Juan Carlos side-eyed Diego.

Diego cocked his head at Juan Carlos. "He's twenty-five. I'm only thirty, and I don't like him."

Juan Carlos made a dismissive sound. They said nothing more as they rode the two floors down. Juan Carlos couldn't help the smile on his face. He didn't feel guilty for calling out Diego. What did worry him was Diego letting his work and his night activities interfere with his personal life. He was happy that Diego was finally showing an interest in someone.

"Get that smug look off your face," Diego growled, stepping off the elevator. "Lead the way."

Juan Carlos strode past Diego. "Get that expression off your face before you get frown lines. He's right in here." Juan Carlos grinned at Diego before opening the door. "I think you'll like who I hired. He's already proven himself to be quite a valuable asset."

They stepped through the door. Diego paused, seeing the young man working diligently at his computer. "You're an asshole. Why didn't you tell me?" Diego whispered softly through his smile.

Juan Carlos whispered back, "You jumped to conclusions, and for the record, I prefer bitch. It suits me better. Now quit acting like a fool and put on your professional face." Juan Carlos cleared his throat. "Alex, I've brought Mr. Sanz here to look at your work."

Alex looked up from the screen. Diego saw joy in his bright brown eyes. He remembered having that passion for work once upon a time. "I have it all right here, Mr. Romero." Alex spun around in his chair and began typing on another computer.

"Juan Carlos," Juan Carlos corrected. "I told you to call me Juan Carlos."

Alex spun in his chair to face them. "I'm sorry, sir, I mean Juan Carlos. Let me pull up the simulations on the big screen for you." He turned back to the computer. With a few keystrokes, the leftmost wall came to life. "As you can see, I ran the simulation over a hundred times, and the results were all the same."

Diego walked over to the wall screen and looked at the results. "These look quite different from the simulations Dr. Wyatt showed me." Juan Carlos joined Diego in studying the screen. "Are these simulations accurate?"

Juan Carlos spoke over his shoulder to Alex. "They are now. Go on. Tell him, Alex."

Alex sucked on his lower lip before answering. "When I looked over the simulations Dr. Wyatt sent up, I found that he had tweaked them to show the results that Dr. Wyatt wanted us to see. There was data missing."

"Really? How?" Diego looked over his shoulder at Alex.

"Every time I ran the simulations, even when I changed the variables, I got the same results," Alex explained. "Then I started looking at the coding for the simulations, and that's when I saw that they were set to deliver the same results no matter what."

Juan Carlos grinned. "I gave him that data first thing this morning. Tell him how long it took you to figure it out and create your own simulation."

Diego turned to look at Alex. Alex's cheeks flushed a slight crimson. "An hour." Alex darted his eyes to Juan Carlos, who gave him a nod to continue. He looked back at Diego. "I would have had the simulation data sooner, but I had to get the missing information from Dr. Wyatt's experiments." Alex went meek. "I hacked his files."

"There was a ton more data that Dr. Wyatt was hiding from us," Juan Carlos justified. "We need to have a conversation with Dr. Wyatt. Alex also found a list of possible candidates for clinical trials."

Rage filled Diego. "What?! Not with these results, he's not."

Juan Carlos gave Alex a smile. "You did a great job, Alex. You did me proud. Shall we summon the good doctor to your office, Diego?"

Diego sighed. "Yes, you did a fantastic job, Alex. Thank you."

Diego liked seeing the bright smile on Alex's face. "I was just doing my job. Is there something else you'd like me to work on?"

"I'll have Dion bring you some Special Projects I'd like you to look at." Juan Carlos motioned for Diego to leave. "Oh, and don't hack my computer."

"He watches some really freaky porn. Like really freaky porn," Diego teased.

"Diego," Juan Carlos warned.

Diego opened his eyes exaggeratedly. "I came across it on his computer one day." Diego gasped. "I was traumatized."

"Diego," Juan Carlos warned again.

"I still have nightmares from what I saw." Alex covered his mouth, trying not to laugh. "That's why I see a therapist four times a month."

"Diego!" Juan Carlos pulled Diego, laughing, from the office. "Oh, you'll pay for that," he muttered to Diego. "You're going to pay dearly."

"It'll have been worth it," Diego laughed.

CHAPTER 7

D R. WYATT WAS FURIOUS THAT THEY HAD
forced him to leave the sanctity of his lab to meet with
Diego and Juan Carlos. He had important work to do. He had
to prepare for the clinical trials of Build and Burn. Yes, he had
already named the miracle drug. If these fools were too blind
to see his brilliance and the potential of his masterpiece, then
he would have to take things into his own hands.

"Why am I here? I have important work to do." Dr. Wyatt
sat down in the chair beside Juan Carlos, annoyance evident
on his bearded face.

Juan Carlos looked across the desk at Diego, a silent com-
munication between the two. "We asked you here because we
have some questions." Diego did his best to keep his voice
level and calm. "Mainly about the simulations and the data
you sent up."

Dr. Wyatt stood. "I don't have time to explain the science
behind my work. I'll have Timmy or Jimmy come up here and
explain it to you."

"Sit your ass down, and answer our questions." Juan Carlos's words were as much a warning as a command. "Truthfully."

Diego waited for Dr. Wyatt to sit. "Now about the simulations and data." Diego looked to Juan Carlos for a moment, then back to Dr. Wyatt. "Our new head programmer ran your simulations with the data you provided. He tested all the variables." Diego looked straight into Dr. Wyatt's eyes, trying to see a hint of the deception. "Do you know what he found?"

Dr. Wyatt scoffed. "That my simulations were sound. Really, did you call me up here just to tell me what a great job I've done? I already knew that."

Juan Carlos did his best to temper his anger. "He found that the simulation programming was tampered with. He also found that we did not have all of the data."

"How could you? Do you realize how dangerous this drug is?" Diego accused.

Dr. Wyatt rolled his eyes. "It is not dangerous. I admit that, yes, I didn't include all of the data." It took every ounce of restraint for Juan Carlos not to wring Dr. Wyatt's neck at how cavalier and condescending he was being. "It wasn't anything that would change the fact that the drug works. You have to break a few eggs to make an omelet."

"How about the fact that it's highly addictive? Or that it destroys the body's ability to build muscle on its own, destroys your liver, and has a twenty-five percent mortality rate?" Diego shot back.

"So, you'll always have customers. I don't see the problem. People will be thin and fit. So, a few people may die? People die every day in the pursuit of the perfect body." Diego couldn't believe the arrogance.

Diego leaned back in his chair, trying to control his anger. "Well, we won't be adding to the numbers. After reviewing the additional data, we will not continue with this project."

"You can't!" Dr. Wyatt narrowed his eyes at Diego. "How did you get the additional data, anyway?" He turned his attention to Juan Carlos. "You hacked my files, didn't you?"

"We retrieved our files. They are our files of the research we paid for, on our servers," Juan Carlos answered coolly.

Dr. Wyatt stood, his body vibrating with anger. "Fine. I'll take my research and go to your competitors. I'm sure one of them won't be as shortsighted as you."

There was no mistaking the satisfaction on Juan Carlos's face. "No. No, you won't. That research belongs to us, and your employment contract has a three-year non-compete clause." Juan Carlos set aside the phone he was discreetly typing on. "No one will touch you or any of our research."

Dr. Wyatt's face turned redder than a fire hydrant. "You can't do this to me! This is my life's work! This is my masterpiece!" Dr. Wyatt turned his attention to Juan Carlos. "You! You did this! You won't get away with this!"

Diego was on the edge of his seat, poised to protect Juan Carlos from Dr. Wyatt. "Dr. Wyatt, please calm down. Just because this didn't pan out doesn't mean we can't get you on a new project that can become your masterpiece. One that doesn't, you know, kill people."

Dr. Wyatt turned his anger toward Diego. "Just so you can pull this on me again? No. In fact, you're not going to do this to me now." Dr. Wyatt slammed his hands down on the desk. "You're going to green-light Build and Burn. Now! You shortsighted man-child!"

It took all of Diego's willpower to control his temper. Diego spoke through clenched teeth. "Dr. Wyatt, I'm formally telling you that you no longer work for DJC. Please, leave my office and exit the building quietly. We will have your personal effects delivered to your home address."

"I'm not leaving here without my research. It is mine, and I'm not leaving here without it," Dr. Wyatt hissed back.

Juan Carlos cleared his throat. "I'm afraid that you are." The office door opened, and two large security guards stepped through. Dr. Wyatt glared back at Juan Carlos. "Gentlemen, please escort Dr. Wyatt out of the building."

The men moved to either side of Dr. Wyatt. "This is not the end of this." One of the guards took him by the arm. "Get your hands off me," Dr. Wyatt spat out, shaking his arm free. "I'm leaving, but just so you know, I will have my revenge. On both of you." Dr. Wyatt stormed out of the office, followed closely by the two guards. "You don't have to follow me, you Neanderthals!" he screamed at them from the hall.

CHAPTER 8

ALEX PRETENDED NOT TO BE DISAPPOINTED that there wasn't a warm plate waiting for him when he got home. It didn't dampen the high he felt from his first day working in Special Projects. He liked the work. He had impressed Juan Carlos and Mr. Sanz. They had given him more important projects to work on.

He wished he had someone here, someone to come home to. Someone he could share his day with. Someone he could tell about figuring out that the simulations were rigged and that there was data missing. He wanted to share with someone how he had saved the day by getting the data and building his own simulations.

More importantly, he wanted to share with someone how proud Juan Carlos was of him, how handsome Mr. Sanz was, and how the two made him laugh when they left his office. That he had an actual office with all the latest gizmos, gadgets, and toys he would ever want to play with.

Alex then realized that he did have somebody. Not someone alive, but someone he talked to, someone that he knew listened. Someone that had always loved him. Someone that was always proud of him. Someone that he knew was looking down at him right now with the biggest smile on her face.

Alex looked up, a smile on his face so big it hurt. "Grandma, I got news." He started pulling food out for dinner. "First off, I'm gay." Alex laughed to himself. "But you already knew that, didn't you? You knew before I did." Alex thought about all the times his grandmother had hinted that she'd love him no matter what until he finally came out to her at sixteen. After that, every time he had news, he started out by telling her that he was gay. It was their private joke.

Alex kept talking to his grandmother as he made his dinner and packed the two brown bags with food. Once he started, he couldn't stop. There was so much he wanted to tell her. To him, it felt like she was right there with him, sitting in her favorite chair, listening intently, smiling and laughing when he did.

Alex was at the sink, washing the dishes. "Okay, I have got to tell you about Mr. Sanz. He is sexy, and it's not because he has this incredible body." Alex chuckled at the imaginary question. "Well, if you have to know, I know he has an incredible body because his clothes are practically painted on." Alex set his plate aside to dry. His mouth crept into a guilty smile. "I also searched the internet for him shirtless."

Alex set the glass he had just cleaned beside the plate. "Anyways, right before he left my office with Juan Carlos today, he," Alex closed his eyes and laughed, remembering the antics, "he just made me laugh. I know it was at Juan Carlos's expense, but it was funny."

Alex dried his hands. "Oh, and his butt." Alex turned and nearly jumped out of his skin when he found Shadow Guardian standing there silently. "How long have you been there? Don't you ever knock?" Alex panted, a hand over his racing heart, trying to catch his breath. Shadow Guardian raised his hand over the kitchen counter, formed a fist, then brought it down, knocking three times. "Smart ass."

"Who were you talking to?" Shadow Guardian asked.

Alex put the dish towel away, glaring at Shadow Guardian's faceless mask. "As if it is any of your business, I was talking to my grandmother." Shadow Guardian's head cocked to one side, then looked around. "She's not here. Not really. She died last year." Alex felt a pang of sadness saying the words.

"I just wanted to share my day with someone and," Alex narrowed his eyes at Shadow Guardian, "why am I explaining this to you? And how did you get in? I didn't open the window."

"I told you to get better locks." Shadow Guardian's answer was as ridiculous as it was infuriating. "In fact, this building could use a lot of repairs. You should talk to the landlord about that."

"Okay, Daddy," Alex snipped. "Don't you think I have? Don't you think we all have? He just threatens us with eviction and no one can risk being kicked out. This is all we can afford." Shadow Guardian's head cocked slightly to the side as if he were listening to someone or something. Alex sighed. "Plus, this building has a few undocumented immigrants, and no one wants to risk them being deported."

"What were you going to tell your grandmother about your boss's butt? I mean, she is waiting for you to finish." Alex thought he saw the outline of a smile in the smoky mask.

"None of your business. That's between me and Grandma." Alex turned and left the kitchen from the other side. "Why are you here? To remind me to get new locks?"

Alex turned and was nearly startled again. He hadn't heard Shadow Guardian follow him into the living room. "That and to make sure you're okay since you won't go to a doctor."

"I'm fine." Alex flopped down on the couch. He tried to sound annoyed, but he was actually touched that Shadow Guardian was checking up on him. "Thank you. You know you don't have to keep checking up on me."

"What if I want to?" Alex was just a little taken aback by the question. "I mean, your apartment isn't really safe."

"Right. The locks." Alex nodded.

"The locks, and don't forget the window." Alex heard the playfulness in Shadow Guardian's voice.

"The window that only you can get through." Alex grinned. If he was reading it right, Shadow Guardian was interested in him, as absurd as it sounded. "I'll have that looked at right away."

Shadow Guardian seemed flustered. He shifted uncomfortably, then turned to leave. "I should go. I have to get back to patrol."

"Same time tomorrow?" Alex ventured. "To make sure I'm safe, that is."

Shadow Guardian turned his faceless head back to Alex. "Yes." Shadow Guardian took another step, then paused. "I'll knock next time."

"I'll leave the window open." Alex watched Shadow Guardian disappear into the darkness of his bedroom. "Or you could use a door!" Alex called out after him.

CHAPTER 9

TURNING OFF HIS TRUCK, JIMMY TURNED TO Timmy. "Are you sure you want to do this? We still have our jobs. We can go back to work at DJC on Monday. If we do this, we're out on our asses."

Timmy's voice was barely louder than a whisper when he answered, "We owe him. Without him, we're nothing."

"We're nothing to him except his scapegoats and lackeys." Jimmy scoffed.

"We're doing important work because of him," Timmy defended, his voice showing irritation at having this conversation again. He and Jimmy had this conversation in one version or another at least once a week. "I don't know what you have against Dr. Wyatt. If you don't like him, why are you still working for him?"

Jimmy wanted to say, *Because you are, and I don't want to leave you. Not with him. Because I've wanted you since I first met you in graduate school. Because no matter where you go, I'll be right there by your side, and you know it.*

"Well? Are you going to answer me?" Timmy asked, his meek voice bringing Jimmy out of his thoughts.

Instead of answering the question, Jimmy said, "We don't need him. We do all the work, and he gets the glory. Something fucks up, and we take the fall. If it weren't for us, Build and Burn wouldn't exist. It was your tweak in the formula that got it to work. I doubt he even knows how to make it."

"You're just jealous. Jealous of his success. You're jealous that he's a great scientist and you're nothing more than a lab assistant, and you probably won't be anything more than that." The words Timmy spat out hurt Jimmy. "You're just jealous that I, that I," Timmy thought before he said the next words, "respect him and not you."

"Too bad he doesn't respect you. He'll never respect you. At least I respect you for who you are," Jimmy shot back.

"Jimmy, I'm tired of having this conversation." Timmy closed his eyes. "You're either with us or against us." He opened his eyes and looked at Jimmy. "Are you against us? Dr. Wyatt and me?"

Jimmy sidestepped a question with one of his own. "What are we going to do for work? Did you think about that? Dr. Wyatt had a non-compete clause. So do we. If we leave DJC, we can't work for three years. Three years. Do you have enough money to survive for three years?"

Timmy shifted in his seat uncomfortably. "Dr. Wyatt does. He'll take care of us."

Jimmy studied Timmy, fidgeting in his seat. He didn't mean to sound as harsh as he did. He needed Timmy to see the truth. "Do you really think that? Do you really think he'll do that? Do you? The man only thinks about himself, and you know it."

Timmy kept looking down at the floor of Jimmy's truck. "He'll take care of me. I know he will."

"Fine." Jimmy couldn't look at Timmy anymore. *Why am I asking him to see that Dr. Wyatt will never love him the way that I would when I won't admit to myself he'll never love me the way he loves Dr. Wyatt?*

"Are you mad at me?" Timmy asked, his voice meek and soft again.

"No." Jimmy lied. *I'm mad at you for not seeing that he'll never love you. I'm mad at you because you can't see that he's using you. I'm mad at you for stringing me along with tiny treats of affection that get my hopes up. I'm mad at myself for letting you do it and not walking away.* Jimmy let out a breath. "Are you sure you want to do this?"

"Yes." Jimmy heard it in his voice, the determination to follow Dr. Wyatt no matter what.

With a heavy sigh, Jimmy said, "Fine, I'm in too. For now, and we don't tell him anything about what we did."

"You won't regret it, Jimmy," Timmy said, opening the door. "Dr. Wyatt will take care of us, and I won't tell him anything. Scout's honor."

"I'm going to regret this," Jimmy mumbled, struggling to get out of his truck.

CHAPTER 10

D R. WYATT SAT SLUMPED IN HIS LOUNGER, ice clinking as he swirled his bourbon in his glass. He had nothing to do. Nothing he could do for three years. All because Diego Sanz and his lackey Juan Carlos were too short-sighted to see his brilliance. So a few people would die. It was a small price to pay for his glory.

Then, to be escorted out of the building, denying him access to his research. His research! To deny him access to his life's work! The gall of it! That research was drenched with his blood, sweat, and tears. Well, not his. Timmy's and Jimmy's, but he supervised. That was just as important. He couldn't be bothered with the actual work.

"Come in!" Dr. Wyatt bellowed when he heard the knock on the door. He knew who it was. Only two people ever came to visit him. "Timmy. Jimmy," Dr. Wyatt said when they entered. Forgoing any other pleasantries, he asked, "How much of my research do you still have access to?"

Jimmy rocked back and forth nervously. "They, uh, locked down all the information the moment you left the lab." Jimmy looked down at the ground. "They escorted us out of the lab five minutes after you left."

Timmy spoke up, his voice soft and timid. "They cleaned out the lab. They took everything that wasn't nailed down. Laptops, tablets, flash drives, and any paper they found." Timmy stepped back when he saw the rage in Dr. Wyatt's eyes. "We couldn't stop them."

"Did you even try?" Dr. Wyatt took a long sip of his drink. He stared intently at Jimmy and Timmy. "Of course not. The two of you are spineless."

"That's not fair." Jimmy thrust his shoulders back and straightened his back. He tried to look intimidating, but it only made the rotund man look bigger. "We're scientists, not street fighters."

Dr. Wyatt slammed the last of his drink. "What you are is worthless. You just let them take everything I worked on for the last five years away." The two men took a step back when Dr. Wyatt stood. "After I took a chance on the two of you. Where would you be if I hadn't? Huh? I'll tell you! Still cleaning rat cages!"

"I, uh, I have a secret backup," Timmy squeaked from behind Jimmy. "I was backing everything up to my home server so I could work at home. Jimmy and I know the formula by heart, too."

Timmy ducked behind Jimmy when Dr. Wyatt came rushing at him. "Why did you wait so long to tell me that?!" Jimmy maneuvered himself between the two. "How much of my work do you have on your servers?!" Dr. Wyatt tried to get around Jimmy, but the big man kept blocking him. "Will you get your fat ass out of my way?!" Dr. Wyatt was getting annoyed with Jimmy's sudden realization that he had a spine.

"Leave him alone. You're scaring him." Jimmy puffed out his chest as best he could.

Dr. Wyatt hated to admit that Jimmy was right. If he wanted his research off Timmy's servers, he'd have to talk sweetly to the scrawny man. He tried to make his voice as calm and soft as possible. "You're right. I'm sorry. Timmy." Dr. Wyatt bit the inside of his cheek to keep from shouting again. "How much of my research do you have backed up?"

Timmy peeked out from around Jimmy. "All of it." He took a cautious step from behind Jimmy. "Please, don't be mad." Dr. Wyatt mentally prepared himself for their screw-up. "We made a few batches of the finished product without your permission."

Dr. Wyatt watched Timmy and Jimmy trade nervous looks. "How much and where are they?" Dr. Wyatt was growing annoyed with pulling this vital information out of these two. He didn't have time for this. "Well?"

"We each have some." Jimmy moved Timmy behind him with his arm. "Five hundred doses."

Dr. Wyatt smiled. He couldn't believe his luck. Dr. Wyatt would have hugged them if he didn't find even the thought of touching them abhorrent. "You have five hundred doses? Do you know what I could do with five hundred doses?"

"No," Jimmy swallowed nervously, "we each have five hundred doses."

Dr. Wyatt's eyes went wide with delight. "Five hundred doses each? Do you know what I could do with a thousand doses?" The delight faded, replaced by anger. "Bring it here! Bring it all here!" The two men turned to leave, only to stop when Dr. Wyatt spoke again. "No! Wait. This will be the first place they look if we're discovered. We need a place no one will think to look."

SHADOW GUARDIAN AND THE THREE BEARS

"Didn't your uncle leave his gym to you? I know you closed it, but don't you still own the building?" Timmy asked meekly.

Dr. Wyatt's eyes darted around as he thought about it. "Yes. Brilliant. I'm glad I helped you think of it. No one would think to look for us in a gym."

Jimmy ran a hand over his ample belly. "Speak for yourself. I go to the gym at least once a year to renew my membership."

Dr. Wyatt ignored Jimmy's attempt at humor. "Let me get the keys. We need to go to the gym."

CHAPTER 11

I T WAS JUST PAST ONE IN THE MORNING WHEN Shadow Guardian stealthily dropped onto the rooftop garden of the penthouse. It was a vibrant, warm oasis of colors in a bland desert of cold grey steel. This luxury was a criminal indulgence as far as Shadow Guardian was concerned. That didn't stop him from appreciating the hibiscus bloom curled up for the night.

Shadow Guardian didn't hear the soft footsteps of the owner of the garden until he was almost on him. "You should see them during the day." Shadow Guardian turned to see Juan Carlos in his sleep clothes, a fluffy robe wrapped tightly around him. "How did the latest enhancements to the suit work?" Juan Carlos rolled his eyes at the thumbs up Shadow Guardian gave him. "Take off that damn suit and talk to me like a human being."

Shadow Guardian started tugging at the seamless suit, making a show of not being able to remove it. "Oh, we're playing games." Juan Carlos put his hand into the pocket of his robe, finding the tiny device there. "Are you going to take your mask off so we can talk?" Again, Shadow Guardian made a show at pulling off his mask. "Really? We're doing this?"

Juan Carlos pressed the button in his pocket. The black and gray swirls on the suit stopped moving, then slowly moved down Shadow Guardian's head, up his arms, and up his legs to the center of his chiseled chest. It swirled into a disc that clung to his smooth skin, leaving Shadow Guardian naked except for a black jock.

Juan Carlos reached out and plucked the disc from Diego's chest. "You know you can wear more than that in that thing. Now, how did the new enhancements to the suit work out?"

Diego grinned. "You know there are easier ways to get me naked. You know, I think we forgot about the stripper market. Can you imagine being able to take your clothes off without losing them?"

Juan Carlos groaned. "Diego, it's late. Can we not do this?"

"Fine. The new enhancements worked great." Diego started walking toward the house, Juan Carlos at his side. "I barely felt the tug when clinging to the sides of buildings. Of course, I could be getting stronger." Diego flexed his bicep.

Juan Carlos yawned. "Save it for the men who didn't raise you as their own. Better yet, save it for Alex."

"Why would I save it for Alex?" Diego quickly changed subjects as they entered the kitchen. "The suit formed about thirty shadow darts and stars before the integrity weakened and needed to charge itself back up."

"I'll have the engineering team look into it and have Alex run a few simulations." Juan Carlos leaned on the breakfast bar as Diego rummaged through the refrigerator for bottled water. "Speaking of Alex, are you going to ask him out as Shadow Guardian or Diego?"

"What? Ouch! Fuck!" Diego hit his head on the refrigerator before standing straight up and turning to face Juan Carlos. "What are you talking about?"

Juan Carlos stifled a yawn. "I'm talking about how you showed up as Shadow Guardian in his apartment two nights in a row. I'm talking about how you were poorly hiding how upset you were when you thought I fired him and how poorly you hid how happy you were when you saw he was our new analyst in Special Projects."

Diego leaned against the closed refrigerator, trying to be nonchalant. "I was concerned about him after that night I rescued him and don't tell me you aren't sweet on him. You made him head programmer of Special Projects. Of course, he's the only programmer."

Juan Carlos sat on one of the barstools. "For now, and I will admit that I am fond of him but not in a sexual way. I see something in him, something that, if nurtured, could grow into something wonderful." Juan Carlos grinned at Diego. "Of course, what you see in Alex is you. The question is as Shadow Guardian or as Diego."

Diego pushed off the refrigerator and took several big gulps of water. "We are not having this conversation. I'm not interested in Alex in that way. He's an employee."

Juan Carlos picked at a loose thread on his robe. "Are you forgetting that I was listening the entire time? By the way, I found out who owns his building." He looked Diego in the eyes. "We do, and before you raise holy Hell, I've already contacted the property management company and put the fear of Juan Carlos in them."

"We're going to need to do a full audit of all of our assets." Diego started for his bedroom. "Too many things that shouldn't are slipping between cracks."

Juan Carlos followed behind Diego. "Right now, your assets are hanging out, and I'm seeing your crack." Diego shook his ass at Juan Carlos. "Save it for Alex. A little bird told me he likes your butt."

"I'm not interested in him." Diego stopped in the doorway to his room. Turning to face Juan Carlos, he said, "He was about to say something nice about my butt, wasn't he?"

Juan Carlos moved on to his room. "Good night. Get some sleep. We have buildings to inspect tomorrow." Juan Carlos stopped in his doorway and called over his shoulder. "Make sure you wear your khakis, the ones that really show off your butt, in case we run into Alex when we inspect his building."

"That's a great idea." Diego then added, before shutting his door, "And I don't like Alex."

"Oh, course not," Juan Carlos mumbled, shutting his door. "And I'm not fabulous in blue."

CHAPTER 12

D R. WYATT'S HEAD THROBBED. THE
morning light stung his eyes. They had spent the better
part of the night cleaning the dust and cobwebs out of the gym.
Well, Timmy and Jimmy had cleaned while Dr. Wyatt had
done the important work. Supervising. It always amazed Dr.
Wyatt that they could dress themselves on their own, let alone
do the complicated work he required of them.

Before they left for the night, Dr. Wyatt had made Timmy
and Jimmy bring all their doses of Build and Burn to the gym,
along with all of his coveted research. These important trea-
sures could not be left in the fumbling hands of imbeciles.
They were like the pompous idiots at DJC, too short-sighted
to see the true potential of his work.

He knew why they had the doses made and then hidden
them away. They were going to betray him. They were going
to use Build and Burn, then pass it off as their own. They
were going to take credit for his work. The idiots made it an
injectable instead of a pill. That's how short-sighted they were.

This was why he was the boss while they were the pathetic underlings. They needed to be reminded of their place in the pecking order.

He would show them. He was going to make sure he took the first dose. After he watched them count the vials for the third time, he put one of the needles in his pocket, then palmed one of the vials. Sliding the needle into his skin, he pressed the single dose into his arm. He would be the first to reap the glory of Build and Burn.

He felt it coursing through his system. It felt like his blood was boiling in his veins. He fell to the floor, his body jerking and jolting about. His nerves exploded under his skin while his muscles tore themselves from his splintering bones. The scream of agony died in his throat right before everything went black.

Now he was awake with his head throbbing and the piercing light from the window stinging his eyes. He picked himself up off the floor. His clothes felt tight on his body. Too tight. He wobbled slightly on his unsteady legs. The throbbing in his head slowly faded away. Things looked clearer than normal. He took an uneasy step.

Hearing the crunch of glass, he looked down to see his broken glasses underfoot. He squinted, then opened his eyes wide, realizing he no longer needed them. That's when he noticed his pant legs were torn and shredded. What shocked him more than that were the bulging muscles that showed through the tatters of his pants.

It took him a moment to realize what had happened, what the drug did to his body. "It worked," he said in awe, raising his arms to see his bulging biceps and defined forearms peeking through his mutilated sleeves. "It fucking worked."

He had to see himself, had to see how his drug had transformed his body. He dashed to his bedroom. He admired himself in his full-length mirror, mesmerized by the rapid change. He didn't recognize the sexy beast looking back at him. He pulled at his clothing, ripping and tearing the fabric that dared to hide his perfect body. He needed to see all of him. When he did, he nearly broke down in tears.

Dr. Wyatt's bearded face was lean and angular. His biceps were huge, at least thirty-five inches around. He had meaty pecs and a six, no, a twelve pack of hard abdominal muscles that peaked through the forest of auburn hair. His legs were defined and bulky. Each cheek of his ass was a perfectly rounded bubble, dusted with red hairs.

Then there was the most unexpected, yet wonderful, benefit—his package, while nothing to be ashamed of before, was now eight inches of hard, thick, and veiny man meat. It jutted out from his groin, swaying as he moved.

He couldn't take his eyes off of his body. Without even thinking about it, he began to touch himself. His hand explored his chest, feeling the hard muscles through his coarse hair. He loved his new body, loved how it felt, loved how it looked.

Dr. Wyatt let go of himself. *No. My first orgasm in this new body won't be like this.*

He turned away from the temptation of the mirror and searched for his phone. Finding it in the remains of his clothes, he took pictures of himself. Thirst traps, ass pics, dick pics, and chest pics. Then he downloaded a few hook-up apps and created profiles, choosing an appropriate picture for each.

Within minutes, he had people hitting him up. He quickly went through the messages, dismissing those not worthy of his attention, those without profiles or even pictures. He wanted a man, not a flake. He wanted someone worthy of him. Someone that could please him properly and satiate the growing desire to climax.

The first so-called man claimed to be an expert dick sucker with no gag reflex. Dr. Wyatt proved him wrong on both points. Answering the door naked, because he no longer had anything that fit, Dr. Wyatt pulled the young muscle boy into the house and pushed him to his knees. The young man barely had his mouth open before Dr. Wyatt was in it.

The young man was pretty. It was a shame that he couldn't live up to Dr. Wyatt's expectations. Dr. Wyatt was pretty sure the lack of air caused the boy to pass out. He wasn't sure if it was the lack of air or his manhood destroying the young man's trachea that caused the young man's death. It didn't matter.

Dr. Wyatt wasn't satisfied. He wanted more, craved more. He needed more. Grabbing the lifeless man by the hair, Dr. Wyatt dragged the body into the kitchen while he searched on his phone for the next man upon whom he would bestow the honor of pleasuring him. What he found, instead, was the next man that would fail him in achieving a real orgasm.

This man, older with thick bulging muscles, claimed to be a power bottom, able to take any man no matter how rough. He showed up, high on poppers, and ready to play. Dr. Wyatt pulled him into the bedroom, leaving a trail of the man's clothes along the way before Dr. Wyatt tossed him onto the bed, face down, ass up.

Dr. Wyatt was on the man's back, and he slammed into the man without mercy. Dr. Wyatt had pushed the man's head into the bed to quiet his screams without care or concern for anything but his own orgasm. The man's body eventually went rigid, then limp.

Dr. Wyatt didn't care. First, the bed frame broke, then the bed itself came apart, then the man's body was being pounded into the floor. Dr. Wyatt heard boards break and bones snap as the crushed, lifeless body was yet another disappointment.

It wasn't until after the third man that Dr. Wyatt realized that none of the men were capable of pleasuring him properly. Dr. Wyatt had him bent over the couch. He needed the man to arch his back more, so he pulled the man back by his shoulders. He pulled the man until his back snapped.

Without the fight of life in him, Dr. Wyatt was able to get him into the proper arch so he could achieve another dissatisfying orgasm. He pushed the body onto the floor, angry that true pleasure eluded him. What use was this magnificent body and this package if he didn't have a true orgasm?

Dr. Wyatt needed someone like him, someone that had his stamina, his strength, and could take his full self. What he needed was someone who had taken Build and Burn, like he had. Someone who would take it willingly. Someone he could control. Someone like Timmy. He needed to see the results on someone with his body type, anyway.

Dr. Wyatt looked around. He couldn't have Timmy come here. He had three dead bodies, a destroyed bed, and was pretty sure his couch was ready to break. He would have Timmy meet him at the gym, but first, he needed clothes. While he was perfectly okay walking around naked, society was not yet so enlightened.

From the three men's belongings, he pieced together something to wear. He found their phones and crushed them so they couldn't be tracked. He went through their wallets, pulling what little cash and their credit cards from them. In the cum pig's wallet, he found the card to a leather store he'd need to pay a visit to.

"Dr. Wyatt? You wanted to see me?" Timmy nervously called, creeping into the darkened gym.

"Yes. I'm so happy to see you, Timmy." Dr. Wyatt's voice came from the darkness. His voice was different from what Timmy remembered. It scared him.

Timmy stepped farther into the shadows, trying to find Dr. Wyatt. "R-really? You said there was something you needed my help with?" Timmy jumped at the sound of something falling. "What did you need?"

"I wanted you to see." Dr. Wyatt moved around the darkness, making sure he got Timmy far enough away from the door and close enough to him. "Build and Burn works."

Timmy moved farther in, his body trembling with fear. "I-it does? How... how do you know?" Dr. Wyatt stepped out of the darkness and into a sliver of light that sneaked through the boarded-up windows. Timmy stood and gasped. "Dr. Wyatt?"

"Call me Wyatt, Timmy." He moved closer to Timmy. "See what it has done for me? Imagine what it could do for you." Dr. Wyatt flexed his muscular biceps.

Timmy took a cautious step back. "What did you do?"

Dr. Wyatt moved closer. He was just out of arm's reach of Timmy. "The same thing you and Jimmy were going to do. I took Build and Burn."

Timmy swallowed hard, wanting to run from the building, but was too scared to move. "W-we, we weren't going to take it. We were stockpiling it for you. We wanted to make sure you had a backup in case things went bad with Mr. Sanz." Timmy glanced back at the entrance, mentally calculating whether or not he could make it out the door before Dr. Wyatt caught him. "Honest."

"No need to lie, Timmy." Dr. Wyatt reached out and snatched Timmy by the arm. Holding him in a bear hug, he lifted the frail young man off the ground. "I know the truth. Don't worry; I'm not mad," Dr. Wyatt said sweetly to the struggling Timmy. "I want you to take a dose. I want you to take the dose so you and I can finally be together." Dr. Wyatt put his mouth next to Timmy's ear. "Like you've always wanted."

Those words took all the fight out of Timmy. Dr. Wyatt loosened his hold on Timmy. "Yes, I know you've had a little crush on me. It's okay. Let me tell you a secret." He sat Timmy back down on the ground. "I was making Build and Burn so you would have the body I wanted, my little honey trap." Timmy turned away from Dr. Wyatt, tears welling up in his eyes. "Come, let's get you that first dose."

"We can finally be together like you wanted. You just have to take one little dose." Timmy turned to see Dr. Wyatt's outstretched hand. He took the offered hand and let him lead him into the back of the gym, where dusty old mats were strewn across the floor. A weight bench sat in the middle of one with a needle on top. Timmy knew what was going to happen. He wanted it to happen. He was doing this so he and Dr. Wyatt could be with each other. That's what he told himself.

"Here, let's get you out of these clothes. Trust me, you don't want to be wearing these when the transformation finishes." Dr. Wyatt pulled the tee shirt off of Timmy. He then sat down on the bench and started undoing Timmy's pants.

Kicking off his shoes, Timmy wordlessly stepped out of his pants, leaving him there in just his cotton briefs in front of the now hunky Dr. Wyatt. "We'll finally be together," Dr. Wyatt spoke to him in a calm, loving tone.

"Is it going to hurt?" Dr. Wyatt ignored Timmy's question. He picked up an alcohol swab and cleaned a spot on Timmy's arm. "Dr. Wyatt, is it going to hurt?" Timmy asked again, trying to swallow down his fear.

Dr. Wyatt intentionally ignored the repeated question. He picked up the syringe and placed the needle tip to Timmy's skin. "I'm not going to lie." A cruel smile crept across Dr. Wyatt's lips. The needle broke the skin. "It's going to hurt like a son of a bitch." Timmy's eyes went wide. He tried to pull away, but Dr. Wyatt's grip was too tight. "Now, now, Timmy. It'll all be over soon." He pushed the liquid into Timmy's veins.

Dr. Wyatt pulled the needle from Timmy's arm. Releasing him, Dr. Wyatt watched with delight as his creation went to work. Timmy opened his mouth to scream, but nothing came out. Timmy clutched his head as he dropped to the floor. Dr. Wyatt saw the fear and terror in Timmy's eyes before he fell to the side, unconscious. Dr. Wyatt wondered if he looked that pathetic when he transformed.

He marveled at how Timmy's skin seemed to bubble as the bones and muscles underneath tore themselves apart and then reformed. Dr. Wyatt stood over the mutating body. "Don't worry, Timmy. I should be back before you wake. I have a little errand to run. Let's hope you're alive when I get back." He left Timmy's transforming body there, bathed in the dingy light.

Dr. Wyatt tolerated the bulldog of a man touching and groping him as he adjusted the leather pants and harness he picked out. The leering lustful looks the squat man gave had amused him. Dr. Wyatt thought the man was going to spontaneously climax when he asked him to try on things, then stripped naked in the middle of the shop before Tyler, the owner, could answer.

"You look really good in a harness." Tyler adjusted the bulldog harness on Dr. Wyatt. "The pants fit perfectly too." Tyler stepped back and admired the tight leather that encased Dr. Wyatt's meaty thighs. "I can't believe this is the first time you've worn leather. You're perfect for it."

"I really didn't have the," Dr. Wyatt paused as he chose his words carefully, "confidence to wear it before. Now, though."

He turned and looked at himself in the mirror. "I'll take it. I'll take all of it."

Dr. Wyatt had nearly cleaned Tyler out of all of his fetish gear and toys by the time he finished. Tyler's grin through his grey speckled beard grew wider and wider as he rang up the items. He grew a little nervous when he told Dr. Wyatt the total. Dr. Wyatt was unphased, pulling out one of the "borrowed" cards of his earlier conquests and handing it over.

"Funny," Tyler said, looking at the name on the card before swiping it. "One of my best customers has the exact same name." Dr. Wyatt frowned. "Is something wrong?"

"I wish you hadn't said that." Before Tyler knew what was happening, Dr. Wyatt had reached across the counter and pulled him from behind the counter, sending Tyler crashing into the wall behind him, merchandise falling all around. "You couldn't just swipe the card."

Tyler struggled to get up. "What the hell, man? Why did you do that?"

Dr. Wyatt grabbed a package of nylon rope from a display. "Which one was your customer? Was it the expert dick sucker?" Dr. Wyatt grabbed Tyler by the arm and twisted it behind his back. Tyler screamed in pain as Dr. Wyatt twisted his other arm to join the other behind his back. "Or was it the power bottom?" Dr. Wyatt began tying Tyler's wrists together. "No, it had to be the other one."

"I don't know!" Fear gripped Tyler. Struggling futilely against his bonds, he winced in pain. "What do you mean 'was'? What did you do to him?"

Dr. Wyatt laughed wickedly. "Let's just say they didn't live up to their titles." Dr. Wyatt began tying Tyler's ankles together. "Be glad that I have a use for you." Dr. Wyatt grabbed a ball gag from the mess on the floor. "Open wide." Tyler clamped his mouth shut and turned his head away to prevent Dr. Wyatt from putting it in. "Either let me put this in your mouth, or I'll break your teeth trying to get it in." Tears of fear streamed down Tyler's cheeks. Opening his mouth, he let Dr. Wyatt put the rubber ball in his mouth and fasten the strap around his head.

Dr. Wyatt stood and looked about. "I'm guessing you have cameras in here. We'll have to destroy that footage." Dr. Wyatt eyed the clothing on the rack. "No need to waste the rest of this."

Dr. Wyatt began gathering any and everything he could. Jocks, vests, leather pants, chaps, and harnesses. He carried them by the bagful to his car. He wrapped Tyler in a set of rubber sheets, then carried him out and locked him in the trunk. Returning to the doomed store, Dr. Wyatt poured every flammable chemical and cleaner around the store.

He was ready to set everything ablaze when he noticed the three neoprene bear hoods behind the counter. All of them were black, but each was highlighted with a different color—one with red, one with yellow, and one with green. He pulled them off the mannequin heads. "These may come in handy." Dr. Wyatt grabbed one of the novelty lighters from the counter and a flier advertising some frivolous Gay Circuit Party. Setting the flier on fire, he dropped it onto the floor, igniting the chemicals before walking out.

CHAPTER 13

ALEX WAS STARTLED WHEN HE OPENED HIS door in the late morning to see Juan Carlos and Mr. Sanz standing there. Alex's stomach immediately twisted in knots. His mind immediately went to the worst-case scenario. He knew they were here to fire him, and they came to his place because they didn't want him making a scene at the office like Dr. Wyatt had. Why else would a CEO and CFO be at his door on a Saturday morning?

"Alex? You live here?" Juan Carlos asked in mock shock. "What a pleasant surprise."

"Yeah." Alex looked uneasily from Juan Carlos to Mr. Sanz to the immaculately dressed woman in a periwinkle dress suit. Remembering his manners, he stepped aside and asked, "Would you like to come in? I'm sorry the place is a bit of a mess."

"Nonsense, I'm sure it's fine." Juan Carlos stepped in. He stopped when he saw electronic parts scattered across every available surface. Juan Carlos covered his heart with his hand. "Hijo de mi alma."

"I'm building a computer," Alex explained. Diego had an amused grin on his face. He moved to Juan Carlos's side and put a hand on his shoulder. "If I would have known you were coming by, I would have cleaned up."

Diego was trying not to laugh. "It's fine. Isn't it, Juan Carlos?" Juan Carlos kept staring. Diego winked at Alex. "Juan Carlos is a bit of a neat freak. He'll be okay in a moment." Diego patted Juan Carlos on the back. "Fight the urge to clean. Fight it. You can do it."

Juan Carlos turned his head toward Diego. "Keep it up, and I won't let you go out tonight," Juan Carlos warned.

"You're so mean. Are you going to send me to bed without dinner, too?" Diego continued to tease. Juan Carlos gave Diego a look that sent a shiver down Alex's spine. "I'll stop."

"Thank you." Juan Carlos looked at Alex. "This is Esmerelda. She runs the property management company we hired to replace the one that obviously has not been doing its job."

"Pleasure to meet you." Esmerelda stepped forward and stuck out her hand for Alex. "As I've been telling all of the residents, we're going to make right what the previous management company failed to do."

"Pleasure to meet you as well." Alex smiled, then frowned. "Wait, you own my building? When did this happen?" he asked Diego and Juan Carlos.

"We've owned the building for some time," Juan Carlos answered, taking a step farther into the apartment. "Like you, it seems to have been overlooked." Juan Carlos ran a finger along a clear stretch of Alex's kitchen counter, then inspected his finger. "Gracias a dios. It's clean."

"Of course, it is." Alex quirked an eyebrow at Mr. Sanz, who was down on one knee, his khaki pants stretched dangerously thin against his ass. "Mr. Sanz, what are you doing?"

"I'm tying my shoes." Diego smiled over his shoulder at Alex.

Juan Carlos put a gentle hand on Diego's shoulder. "Dear, you're wearing loafers."

"Those two. They've been like that since I met them." Esmerelda sighed.

"What exactly is going on here? Why are you here?" Alex asked, confused, not sure who to pay attention to.

"We're going to all the residents and apologizing for how run down the building has become," Diego answered, standing and stretching. "We wanted to reassure them that with the renovations, we aren't raising the rent or trying to kick them out."

"Also, we're introducing them to Esmerelda." Juan Carlos playfully smacked Diego when he turned his stretch into a flex. "Stop that."

"My cousin Freddy is going to be the building manager." Esmerelda took Alex by the arm. "He's an artist and an amateur boxer. I love him to death, but he can be, um, single-minded at times." Esmerelda sweetened her voice. "If you could keep an eye on him for me, I'd appreciate that." Esmerelda perked up. "He's single, by the way."

"Alex will be very busy with work. Very busy. He's going to be starting a big project at work," Diego blurted quickly.

"He is? I wasn't aware of that." Juan Carlos smiled mischievously.

Diego answered through a clenched-teeth smile. "Yes, he is."

Esmerelda patted Alex's hand. "Well, Freddy needs a friend in the area and someone to keep him on track. Oh, just a heads up: we'll be renovating the laundry room first, so if you have any laundry to do, please do it by Monday."

Alex pulled away from Esmerelda. "What? You can't do that." Alex sucked on his lower lip as the three looked at him, waiting for an explanation. "Pat sleeps in there some nights."

"Who is Pat?" Esmerelda looked at Juan Carlos, then back at Alex. "Alex?"

"They are a homeless teen. They crash in the laundry room most nights," Alex answered reluctantly.

"We can't have a homeless teen crashing in the laundry room. We'll have to find them a place to stay," Esmerelda pronounced. She tapped her well-manicured finger to her lips. "I have it. Tio Pepe."

"I don't think alcohol is the answer." Juan Carlos cupped Diego's head. "Ouch, what was that for?"

"Tio Pepe runs a halfway house for troubled Queer youth," Esmerelda explained. "He helped me with my drag and then with my transition." She smiled proudly. "I was a fierce performer. No one could outdo me except," Juan Carlos cleared his throat, "anyways. Tio Pepe can help Pat. Do you think you could arrange for me to meet them?"

The fact that Esmerelda had shared her story and picked up on Pat's pronouns so quickly put Alex at ease. "I can talk to them, but I can't guarantee anything."

Esmerelda smiled. "That's all I can ask. We have other buildings we have to visit, but I'll leave you my number. Call me with a good time to meet them." She handed Alex her card.

"If Diego is done ... being Diego. We need to go." Juan Carlos patted Alex on the back. "We'll see you at work Monday." Juan Carlos gave Diego a side-eye. "For that big project Diego has for you."

"Remember, you're going to be really, really busy with it. Really busy." Diego gave Alex a wink.

Alex wasn't sure what to make of Diego's wink. "Okay, yeah. I'll see you on Monday." Alex shut the door after them. "What was that about?"

CHAPTER 14

D R. WYATT IGNORED TYLER'S SOBS WHILE HE
checked the lock on the chain that tethered his collar
to the wall. Tyler had run the gambit of begging and pleading
for his life, promising not to tell anyone to sexually gratifying
Dr. Wyatt. Now, with his arms and legs freed, Tyler lay curled
up on the floor, fearing for his life.

"Pathetic." Dr. Wyatt sneered before leaving the crumpled
and broken man. He had business to take care of. He needed
another injection. He needed to check on Timmy. He needed
to get the dead bodies out of his house. More importantly, he
needed to climax.

Dr. Wyatt could handle the injection. Timmy would help
with the rest. That is, if he survived. There was that pesky mortality rate of Build and Burn. If Timmy didn't survive, there
was always Jimmy. If Jimmy didn't survive, well, there was
a whole city of malleable people available until he got it right.

Dr. Wyatt pushed the needle into his skin. The nagging
craving that was quietly eating away at his patience faded

away as the liquid coursed through his veins. He let out a sigh of relief as the drug made its way through his system. With that done, he pulled the needle out and turned his attention to Timmy's still unconscious body sprawled out on the mats.

A salacious smile spread across Dr. Wyatt's face as he got closer to the passed-out Timmy. His scarecrow reject of a body was a thing of the past. Timmy now had toned, well-defined legs and arms, a perfect swimmer's chest that tapered in a perfect V-shape along his hard, smooth stomach with its six hard ridges.

"My, don't you look just as sweet as honey?" Dr. Wyatt licked his lips, his cock stirring to life in his leather pants. "That is, if you survived." He watched the slight rise and fall of Timmy's breathing. "What a tasty morsel you turned out to be." Timmy began to stir, mumbling something Dr. Wyatt could not hear.

Dr. Wyatt dropped down to one knee. Putting a caressing hand on Timmy's chest, he gently nudged Timmy and said, "Wake up, my sweet honey bear," Dr. Wyatt said, his voice uncharacteristically soft and gentle. Timmy stirred but did not wake. "Timmy, wake up."

Timmy tried to roll away, but Dr. Wyatt's strong hand kept him in place. "Five more minutes. I don't want to get up," Timmy whined sleepily. Dr. Wyatt was torn between throttling the insolent whelp and curling up next to him. "I don't feel like going to work for that asshole, Dr. Wyatt."

Uncontrollable rage boiled up in Dr. Wyatt. Shaking Timmy harder, he snarled, "Wake your pathetic ass up now." Dr. Wyatt was seething now. "Get your ass up now!" Dr. Wyatt stood so he was looming over Timmy now.

Timmy yawned sleepily and stretched. He yawned and blinked his eyes open. "My head hurts, and my body feels funny," Timmy groaned, rubbing the sleep from his eyes. He squinted up at Dr. Wyatt. "What are you wearing? Is that a harness?" Timmy clumsily stood up. He eyed Dr. Wyatt hungrily. He reached out to touch him, but Dr. Wyatt caught him by the wrist. "You look really good in leather."

"I'm an asshole?" The heat of anger faded from Dr. Wyatt's voice as he took in Timmy's body again. "You look really good. Good enough to eat." Dr. Wyatt's nostrils flared. There was a strange scent in the air. "My, my Build and Burn did a wonderful job on you."

Timmy's eyes brightened with excitement. "Really? I want to see. Can I see? Where's a mirror?"

Letting go of his wrists, he motioned with his head to the wall behind Timmy. "Over there."

Timmy turned. He froze when he saw the distant reflection. Timmy stepped toward the filthy mirror, one hand going to the stone-chiseled features of his face, not believing what he was seeing. "Is that me?" When he was close enough to the mirror, Timmy reached out and touched his reflection. "I'm... I'm beautiful."

Dr. Wyatt appeared in the reflection behind Timmy. He slipped an arm around Timmy's slender waist and rested his other hand on Timmy's hip. Kissing Timmy's neck, he said, "Yes, you are. We should celebrate our success."

"What did you have in mind?" Timmy leaned back into Dr. Wyatt. He closed his eyes and enjoyed the feel of Dr. Wyatt on his skin.

Dr. Wyatt moved his hand down to grip the hard outline of Timmy's dick in his jockeys. "I think you know. That is, if you would want to celebrate with an asshole." Dr. Wyatt's lips grazed Timmy's ear as he spoke. "Is that what you really think of me?"

Timmy laughed softly. "Yes, and you know you are." Timmy covered Dr. Wyatt's hand with his to keep him from taking it away. "I still wanted you, though. I still want you." Timmy turned in Dr. Wyatt's arms. He ran a hand through Dr. Wyatt's chest hair, then over the black leather. "You look really good in leather," Timmy purred. "Do you think I could get some?"

Dr. Wyatt wasn't even aware his hand moved from Timmy's hip to his ass. "I brought some back for you to try on, but first, we need to get you out of these." Dr. Wyatt patted Timmy's ass.

Timmy tried to move away, but Dr. Wyatt tightened his grip with a feral growl. Timmy flashed him a coy smile. He roughly pulled Timmy against him. Dr. Wyatt's nostrils flared with the intoxicating scent in the air. He released his grip. He watched Timmy with hungry eyes as he stepped away, moving with a dancer's grace.

Timmy turned his back to Dr. Wyatt. Looking over his shoulder, he gave Dr. Wyatt a wink. Hooking his thumbs in his briefs, Timmy wiggled his ass as he teasingly lowered his briefs just slightly. Dr. Wyatt let out a snarl. That made Timmy grin even wider. With a dramatic flair, Timmy bent at the waist, pulling his underwear down his toned legs.

"Like what you see?" Timmy shook his ass at Dr. Wyatt.

Dr. Wyatt wasn't sure what came over him when he lunged for Timmy's ass. "Yes! Give it to me!"

Timmy quickly stood and evaded Dr. Wyatt's lustful attack. Playfully he said, "Not so fast, my sexy Papa Bear." Timmy stepped close to Dr. Wyatt. Running his tongue over his lips, he looked down Dr. Wyatt's heaving chest, then back to his sexually crazed eyes. "Let's enjoy this. Kiss me."

"Give me some of that sweet honey." Pulling Timmy against him, Dr. Wyatt shoved his tongue into Timmy's mouth. His other hand went immediately to Timmy's tight and toned, muscled butt and began kneading the not-so-tender flesh.

Timmy ran his fingers through the forest of fur on Dr. Wyatt's body. Timmy moved down to work open the front of

Dr. Wyatt's pants. Finally clearing the path to the treasure Timmy sought, he slipped his hand down the front of Dr. Wyatt's pants. Wrapping his fingers around the thick hard meat that strained to be freed, Timmy let out a soft moan.

Timmy pulled away from the kiss, moving down to find Dr. Wyatt's nipple. Timmy stroked Dr. Wyatt's package while he chewed on his pectoral. "Fuck yeah. Chew that nipple," Dr. Wyatt growled, moving a hand to the back of Timmy's head. Timmy chewed, feeling Dr. Wyatt's cock grow impossibly hard under his hand. "I need you on me."

Pulling his hand from Dr. Wyatt's pants, Timmy allowed the hand on the back of his head to push him down onto his knees. Timmy looked up with his impish grin at Dr. Wyatt. He worked the skin-tight pants down. Dr. Wyatt's hard and thick manhood bounced free in front of Timmy. He licked his lips at the sight.

"Think you can handle it?" To Timmy, it wasn't a question. It was a challenge. "Well?'

Timmy gripped Dr. Wyatt's penis. "Easily. Let me show you," he said, stroking Dr. Wyatt.

Timmy took Dr. Wyatt's hard-on into his mouth, his lips brushing over the fat crown. Timmy swirled his tongue around the mushroom head, making Dr. Wyatt toss his head back and let out a rumble. He gave Timmy an uncharacteristically gentle nudge with his hand. "Fuck, yeah. Take it all."

Timmy was a man of his word, easily sliding his lips down the veiny hard flesh. Timmy didn't stop until he had all of Dr. Wyatt down, his nose buried in Dr. Wyatt's fiery red pubic hair, inhaling the musky scent. Dr. Wyatt growled. "Damn, you can. What other skills are you keeping from me?"

Timmy's answer was pulling back until just the head was on his tongue, then shoving all of Dr. Wyatt back down his throat. Dr. Wyatt let out a growl of praise. Timmy pulled back and played with the tip. This time, Dr. Wyatt let out a sound that was a mix of annoyance and enjoyment.

Timmy covered the hand Dr. Wyatt had on the back of his head with his own and pushed. "You think you can handle it rough? Let's see." Dr. Wyatt let out a throaty chuckle. Dr. Wyatt pulled Timmy roughly back down to the base of his flesh. He held him there, waiting for Timmy to choke and fight to pull off. Timmy didn't. "I guess you can."

Timmy dropped his hand from the back of his head and let Dr. Wyatt take control. "No turning back now, my sweet honey pot." Dr. Wyatt rammed into Timmy's hungry mouth without any concern for Timmy other than his usefulness in bringing an orgasm.

Timmy willingly let Dr. Wyatt abuse his mouth and throat for nearly half an hour before Dr. Wyatt pushed him off. "I want to see if that ass is as sweet as your mouth." Dr. Wyatt pulled his pants off and tossed them to the side while Timmy watched with a proud smirk on his face.

Timmy wiped the spittle from his face with the back of his hand. "Do you think you can handle it?" Timmy asked cockily, flipping over onto all fours so he was facing the mirror wall. He wanted to watch himself finally get fucked by Dr. Wyatt. "Let's see what you got, Papa Bear."

Dr. Wyatt dropped down behind Timmy. "Arrogant little fuck," Dr. Wyatt grumbled. "I'm going to teach you a lesson. Let's see how you take this."

Timmy cooed at the feel of Dr. Wyatt at his hole. He purred when he felt him push in and make his way into him. Timmy arched his back and rolled his shoulders. "Damn, I love the way you feel in me."

Dr. Wyatt ignored Timmy's words. He was focused solely on sinking balls deep into that tight, warm hole. Once his hips rested against Timmy's hips, Dr. Wyatt let out a sigh that was a mix of relief and satisfaction. He took in a deep breath and exhaled. Dr. Wyatt slapped Timmy's ass. Then, grabbing both of Timmy's hips, he said, "Time to teach you a lesson in respect." Dr. Wyatt went full force at Timmy.

Dr. Wyatt gave no quarter, and Timmy didn't ask for it. Each rapid forward thrust by Dr. Wyatt was met with Timmy's swift bounce back. The sound of hard fleshy smacks echoed through the abandoned gym, punctuated with Timmy's pleas to be fucked harder and deeper.

An hour later, after Dr. Wyatt had had Timmy on his back, his side, on top riding him, Dr. Wyatt had Timmy back on all fours again. His balls were on the cusp of exploding. He just needed that one little something to set him over the edge. Dr. Wyatt grabbed Timmy by the hair and pulled Timmy back until he could whisper in Timmy's ear.

"You're nothing more than a hole to me. That's all I'll ever think of you as and all you'll ever be to me." Dr. Wyatt felt it when the words hit Timmy. His body tightened, then slumped with shame and embarrassment. A moment later, Dr. Wyatt's dick exploded into Timmy.

After a half dozen or so manic pumps into Timmy, Dr. Wyatt pushed him down and thrust hard into Timmy. Dr. Wyatt pulled out and stood, happy that he was finally satisfied. He looked down at Timmy sprawled on his stomach on the floor, white sticky mess leaking from him. Dr. Wyatt turned away, his desire for Timmy fading away. He snatched Timmy's old briefs off the floor.

"We need to get you new clothes," Dr. Wyatt said, cleaning himself with Timmy's underwear. "Something I brought should fit." He tossed the soiled underwear on top of Timmy. "Wipe up, and we'll have my new pet dress you."

Timmy sighed. He rolled over onto his butt and watched Dr. Wyatt slide himself into his leather pants. "Yes, sir, Dr.

Wyatt." He looked down at his own neglected piece. "Whatever you say, Dr. Wyatt."

"Don't call me Dr. Wyatt." Dr. Wyatt adjusted himself in his pants before zipping them up. He grinned sinisterly. "Call me, Papa Bear."

"Yes, Papa Bear." Timmy began wiping himself with his jockeys, hoping what he heard was lust in Papa's voice.

"We should call Jimmy. Have him bring us some food." Papa Bear was lacing up his boots.

"Yes, Papa Bear." Timmy stood, his erection slowly deflating. "Anything else?"

"Yes, we have some bodies to dispose of." Timmy laughed, then realized Papa wasn't joking. "Bodies?"

CHAPTER 15

TIMMY SCROUNGED AROUND IN HIS DIS-
carded clothes for his phone. He could hear Dr. Wyatt,
no, Papa Bear, in the main room, yelling at someone to
stop crying. *They probably deserve it. Anyone who disap-
points Papa Bear deserves exactly what they get,* Timmy
rationalized.

Finding his phone, Timmy tuned out the berating in the
other room. He sent Jimmy a text, ordering him to get his ass
to the gym and to bring 20 pizzas, plenty of soda, and wings.
What did they care about mundane things like calories? They
had Build and Burn, and soon Jimmy would too. They would
be fit and sexy forever.

Timmy strode into the main room, hands running over
his naked body. He was loving his new tight and toned, sexy
body. He saw Papa Bear holding a man up in the air, shaking
him violently as the man cried through a ball gag. Timmy
crossed the room and placed a hand on Papa Bear's shoulder.

"Papa bear, I texted Jimmy to bring us something to eat." Timmy turned his attention to the wailing man Papa was holding off the ground. Timmy asked in a syrupy thick sweet voice, "What do we have here? Something for me to play with when you're busy?"

Cruel amusement filled Papa's voice. "He was the owner of the leather store I got all our stuff from before it mysteriously burned down." Papa Bear shook the man again. "He won't stop crying so he can fit you with your leather."

"Why don't you let me try?" Timmy reached up and touched Tyler's face. "Sometimes, you just need a little sweetness, a little *honey*." Papa dropped Tyler to the ground. "Come on, don't you want to see how I'd look in leather?"

Tyler looked at Timmy. The fear and terror on Tyler's face morphed into adoration. He tried to say something through the ball gag. "Here, let me." Timmy carefully removed the ball gag from around Tyler's head. "There, that's better. Now, what were you saying?"

Tyler moved his jaw around, working out the stiffness. He grinned stupidly at Timmy. "Yes, I'd like to see you in leather very much. I'd be honored to fit your leather."

Timmy laughed softly. "Of course, you will." Timmy nodded to Papa Bear. "I'd like to have a little color in my leather." Papa Bear brought over a few of the bags of leather clothing. "Yellow, if you have it."

Tyler began rummaging through the bags. "You know that yellow is the color of—"

"Honey," Timmy finished for Tyler. "It's the color of honey."

Jimmy was breathing heavily when he entered the gym carrying all the food. It was a struggle to get in the door, but he had managed. He needed a place to rest and air conditioning, neither of which the musty old gym had. When he messaged Timmy to come help him, he cryptically answered, and now he and Dr. Wyatt were nowhere to be seen.

"Hello?" Jimmy called out, trudging farther into the gym. He stopped when he noticed the man chained by the collar to the wall. "What the fuck?" Jimmy almost dropped everything and ran, but then he heard a familiar voice.

"Hey, Jimmy." Jimmy's blood ran cold when he saw who had called his name. It was Timmy, standing in the door to the back rooms, but it wasn't the Timmy he knew. "Like what you see?" Timmy made his way across the room, his hips swaying hypnotically.

"You took it, didn't you? Why? It wasn't safe. It's not safe," Jimmy accused, his voice all but a whisper.

"Safe enough. Don't you like what you see?" Timmy's voice was light-hearted. He took the food from Jimmy's trembling arms and set it on a nearby weight bench.

Jimmy took it all in. Timmy was wearing a double ring yellow harness, two yellow armbands, black chaps, and a yellow striped jock. Timmy spread his arms and turned, showing Jimmy his perfectly sculpted bare ass. Jimmy couldn't deny he liked what he saw. It also scared the shit out of him.

"Yes, but I liked how you looked before, though," Jimmy choked out.

"That scrawny body?" Timmy laughed. He reached out and played with the collar of Jimmy's shirt. "I like this body much more." Timmy began unbuttoning Jimmy's shirt. "I can't wait to see what Build and Burn does for you."

"I'm not taking it," Jimmy protested weakly. "Dr. Wyatt did this, didn't he?" Jimmy let Timmy remove his shirt.

"Timmy, come with me. We can try to reverse the effects before it gets too bad."

Timmy's laugh sent chills down Jimmy's spine. "Why would I want to reverse it?" Timmy ripped open Jimmy's undershirt. "Oh, and don't call me Timmy." Taking Jimmy's meaty hand, he pulled Jimmy toward the back. "I'm Honey Bear now."

Letting himself be led, Jimmy mouthed the name over and over. "Honey Bear. I, uh, I like it."

"So do I. Hello, Jimmy." Papa's voice broke Jimmy's trance-like state.

Jimmy swallowed hard. "Dr. Wyatt? You took it, too?"

"Of course. You were always a bright one. It's a wonder Build and Burn ever got developed with that brilliance in the lab." Jimmy turned his attention back to Honey, watching him fill a syringe with the experimental liquid.

"Be nice, Papa." Honey glared at Papa before turning kind eyes back on Jimmy. "Don't mind him; he's just grouchy because he's hungry."

"I thought we were going to get this place set up first," Jimmy said, letting Honey swab a spot on Jimmy's arm. "You know, get electricity and air conditioning." Jimmy's mind screamed for him to yank his arm away from Honey Bear, but his body did nothing. "What are you doing?" he asked when he saw Honey Bear take the needle from Papa Bear.

"Sshh. Just relax." Honey pushed the needle into Jimmy's arm. He pushed the liquid into Jimmy. "I wonder what kind of bear you'll be."

Jimmy watched the needle be pulled from his arm. He just stared in disbelief at the spot where he let Honey inject him with an experimental medication that obviously had changed more than their bodies. Why had he done that? Why? He had to get out of here, away from them, and get medical attention.

Jimmy tried to take a step back. That's when the burn started. His body ignited with a flameless fire. The pain was so intense that Jimmy fell to his knees, screaming a soundless scream. He clawed at his skin. He looked about, catching glimpses of Papa and Honey grinning at him right before everything went black.

CHAPTER 16

ALEX STEPPED OUT OF THE SHOWER, FEELING good about the day. He finished building the computer for little Chris. He had introduced Esmerelda and Pat, and though they didn't go with Esmerelda, the two really bonded. Alex had a good feeling that Pat would be off the streets soon.

Wiping the steam from the mirror, he debated shaving the barely there scruff off his chin. He wasn't going out, but if the past two nights were any indication, he'd be getting a visitor. A mysterious, sexy, goofy visitor that he was going to have strange, awkward, and silly conversations with.

There was a major possibility that Shadow Guardian wouldn't show. If he did, Alex wanted to be ready. That was why he fussed with his hair for twenty minutes and spent another thirty picking out his clothes. Then, after turning off every light in his apartment except for one lamp, he sat down on the couch to watch television while he waited.

"You're late," Alex joked when he heard the rap of knuckles on wood. "Did you get my note?"

"Cute." Alex heard the slight hint of amusement in his voice. "This window is locked unless you're Shadow Guardian." Alex chuckled to himself. "What if it wasn't me who read that note?"

"Then they would have thought the window was locked because they weren't Shadow Guardian." Alex muted the television and stood to face him. "It worked, didn't it? No one but you came through my window."

"That's not how it works." Shadow Guardian folded the note up and pressed it to his side. Alex watched the suit come alive and surround the paper. "You know that."

"Anyways, why are you late?" Shadow Guardian cocked his head in confusion. "I expected you an hour ago. I was starting to worry," Alex teased.

Shadow Guardian stepped closer to Alex. "There's no need to worry about me. I can take care of myself. If you have to know, I had to check out a suspicious fire that happened today."

Alex took a step closer. "Had to? Or wanted to?"

Shadow Guardian moved again. He and Alex were nearly chest to chest. "Both. Like coming to check up on you."

Alex shook his head in disbelief. "Why? I mean, you're Shadow Guardian. Shadow fucking Guardian. I'm just, well, me."

"Yes, you're that brave, bright light that goes around helping people just because." Shadow Guardian cupped Alex's face. "I'm just some muscle-bound lunkhead in a fancy suit hiding in the dark."

"You're not a lunkhead, but you are goofy." Alex put his hand on top of Shadow Guardian's. "I... I really wish I could kiss you right now."

Shadow Guardian took his hand from Alex's face. Walking around Alex to the coffee table, he took the remote control and turned the television off and then the lamp. Alex turned in the dark to find himself colliding with Shadow Guardian. There was a strange sound, like the skittering of tiny feet.

Shadow Guardian put his arms around Alex. "That's one wish I can make come true."

Alex was shocked when he felt the press of lips on his own. Shadow Guardian was kissing him. Hesitantly, he put his arms around Shadow Guardian's neck and surrendered to the moment. The kiss was gentle and sensual. It made Alex's toes curl and rushed the blood to his groin. Fleetingly he wished for something a bit naughtier when Shadow Guardian pulled away.

"I shouldn't come back here. You deserve more than this. More than I can give you." Shadow Guardian's voice was deep and throaty. He stroked Alex's cheek with the back of his hand. "You deserve your Prince Charming."

"Prince Charming is a fairytale. I want something real." Alex took Shadow Guardian's hand, refusing to let him go. "You made one wish come true. Make this one come true." Shadow Guardian felt the stab of pain in his heart before Alex said the words. "I wish we could be together."

"That's one wish I can't make true. No matter how much I want to, I can't." Soulful agony resonated in his words.

"Then give me this. Let me fall asleep in your arms." Alex felt the hesitation in Shadow Guardian's body. "Please," Alex pleaded.

"Okay, but just an hour." Shadow Guardian hugged Alex close. "No funny business."

"I would never." Alex pulled back, offended.

Shadow Guardian took Alex by the hand. "Not you. I was talking to the annoying little voice in my head."

CHAPTER 17

THE SWEET SMELL OF THE NIGHT BLOOMS PER-
fumed the air of the rooftop garden. Diego sat alone in
his jock on the stone bench, listening to the bubbling fountain,
reflecting on his evening. He had kissed Alex and held him
until he fell asleep. He hated that he could not spend the night
so that he could see Alex when he first woke up.

He knew Juan Carlos was watching him, hidden in the lush
foliage. He'd stay there, among the leaves and flowers, wanting
to come out and comfort Diego, to put his arms around Diego
and hold him—to tell him everything would be okay. Then he'd
admonish Diego for being naked again, and in the garden, of
all places.

Diego sighed, knowing he couldn't keep Juan Carlos at
bay for much longer. Besides, he needed one of Juan Carlos's
warm hugs. The sooner it was done, the sooner they could get
down to business. It was time to take his medicine with the
spoon full of sugar.

"You can come out—ow!" Diego rubbed the back of his head where Juan Carlos smacked him. "Joder! What was that for?"

"Language," Juan Carlos scolded. Juan Carlos's robe flowed around him, reminding Diego of days long past. "Stop being an idiot and put some clothes on."

"Cut me some slack. I told Alex I couldn't see him anymore," Diego grumbled. Juan Carlos cupped Diego's head again. "Ouch! Why did you do that?"

Juan Carlos sat down. "Because you didn't tell Alex anything. Shadow Guardian did."

"I am Shadow Guardian. It's going to really suck seeing him at work." Diego rested his head on Juan Carlos's shoulder.

Juan Carlos rolled his eyes. "How hard did I hit you? You are not Shadow Guardian. Shadow Guardian is not a real person. You are Diego Sanz." Juan Carlos leaned his head on top of Diego's. "You just have to get your head out of your ass."

"Why are you being so mean to me? I've got a broken heart," Diego whined.

"You've got a broken head. You know you couldn't have dated him as Shadow Guardian, but as Diego Sanz, well, you might just have a chance," Juan Carlos chided.

"I'm his boss. I can't date him. It's like sexual harassment or something like that." Diego pouted.

"Hijo, we can find a way. Now, if you're done being an idiot, what did you find out about the fire?" Juan Carlos nudged Diego off his shoulder.

"It was definitely arson, but from what I overheard the cops saying, they are looking at the owner, but I don't think it's him." Diego shivered. "It's cold out here."

Juan Carlos sighed. "You're naked on a stone bench. I swear sometimes. Whatever, anyways, why don't you think it was the owner?"

Diego held up a finger. "The fire was started in the middle of the day. The owner's car was still there." He held up another finger. "That's really all I got."

Juan Carlos stood, wrapping his flowing robe around him tightly. "I'll see if we can hack into the police files and dig up some more. It's getting late. We should go to bed." Juan Carlos cupped Diego's chin. "And hijo, if I catch you naked in my garden again, I'm going to take my hedge clippers to you."

"I'm not naked." Diego stood. "I'm wearing a jock."

Juan Carlos patted Diego's cheek. "You need to wear more than those man-panties out here. You're leaving butt prints everywhere. It's like you're marking your territory." Juan Carlos started walking away. "I hope you left a butt print on Alex. Remember Freddy moves into his building soon."

"No, I didn't leave a butt print on Alex!" Diego scowled at Juan Carlos's retreating back before rushing to catch up with him. "And tell Esmerelda that Alex is off limits!"

"No." Juan Carlos gave Diego an impish grin before closing the sliding glass door on him. Juan Carlos turned away with a flourish of his robe, moving behind the kitchen island when Diego came in. Juan Carlos asked, "Did the door shut because you were too slow to act?" Diego scowled at Juan Carlos. "Oh, look." Juan Carlos picked up a lone cookie off a plate on the counter. "The last chocolate chip cookie. Aren't they your favorite?"

"Juan Carlos, don't," Diego warned. Juan Carlos took a bite of the cookie. "Animal."

Juan Carlos brushed the crumbs from his mouth. "That is why, if you want something, you should snatch it up." Juan Carlos pulled a wrapped napkin from his robe pocket and handed it to Diego. "Here, it wasn't the last cookie, but it could have been. Remember that."

"Yes, Mamacita. Lesson learned." Diego took the cookie. Diego took a bite of the cookie. "Have you hide and protect the last cookie until I'm ready to eat it."

Juan Carlos sighed. "Qué vergüenza. Why do I even bother?"

"Because you love me?" Diego finished the last of his cookie. "Oh, and because I turned your tip money into a tech startup that we sold for a couple million that we used to start our now billion-dollar company."

"Yes," Juan Carlos paused dramatically, "but when will I get to hear the pitter-patter of little feet?"

Diego shrugged. "I did bring that twink home a couple of times. His feet were pretty little, but, oh my God, his—"

Juan Carlos remembered the brat. He gritted his teeth at Diego. "He was a rude little snot. He kept acting like I was the help."

"Yeah, I might have been just a tiny bit responsible for that. I sort of told him you were the maid because it sounded cooler than I live with this old guy that raised me," Diego said sheepishly.

"Diego." Diego took a cautious step back when Juan Carlos said his name. "I'll give you a choice." Diego took another backward step, ready to run. "Which beating do you want first? The one for calling me the maid or the one for calling me old?"

Diego did an exaggerated yawn and stretch. "Would you look at the time? I should really get to bed. Early morning tomorrow. Good night!"

Juan Carlos allowed himself a secret smile at Diego's nearly naked body fleeing. "I did something right raising that boy."

CHAPTER 18

JIMMY WOKE UP ON THE GYM MAT, HIS HEAD throbbing. He struggled to get up. Blinking away the sleep from his eyes, he heard the unmistakable sound of moaning. He looked over to see Dr. Wyatt, no, Papa, sitting naked with Timmy, no, Honey, bouncing up and down on his cock. He watched to the bitter climactic end.

That was when they noticed Jimmy standing there, naked. Honey had smiled sweetly, as if he hadn't just ridden Papa for the last hour while he laid unconscious on the floor. Honey came over and began running his hands over Jimmy's meaty, hairy chest. "Look at you, all muscly and cuddly. You're like a big ole teddy bear."

They called him that now. Jimmy liked it, especially when Honey said it. He wasn't the big lumbering man, well, he was still big and lumbering. He was thick with muscle instead of fat. While he didn't have the ripped body of Papa or the defined muscles of Honey, he had them. He had them with a rich forest of black chest hair that trailed down to a thick ramrod and bull balls.

Honey led him to the chained man in the other room. With a simple touch, Honey had the chained man begging to please him. They had dressed Teddy in leather shorts and a Y harness that crossed his chest and back. He was admiring himself in one of the mirrors when he realized the lights were on and the air conditioning was going.

"I hacked into the electric company's computers and got the power turned back on. The water company, too," Honey had boasted proudly.

Then Papa told them to get ready. They had to take care of something at his house. Teddy had almost thrown up when he saw the broken and bloodied bodies of the naked men in Papa's house. They wrapped the men in bed sheets and carried them to Teddy's truck under the cover of night.

They drove to the Morgan City dump, just outside of town. Papa insisted they wear the bear masks he had liberated from Tyler's leather shop. Papa had put on the red and black one. Honey, of course, took the yellow. That left Teddy with the green accented neoprene mask. Teddy had grumbled about it, but knew they had to hide their faces from prying eyes. Human and electronic.

He had expected some sort of hindrance when they got to the dump, but they found none—no guards or even a gate. Teddy figured it was because you had to go through North Side, and no one who didn't have to went through North Side. Even with Build and Burn flowing through his system, Teddy cringed about going to this part of town.

After dumping the bodies, they headed back to what Teddy assumed was their new home. As soon as they got back, Papa and Honey took another injection of Build and Burn. Teddy had noticed them growing increasingly agitated as the night went on. Papa had ordered them to rest up. They had plans to make in the morning, and he sent Honey and Teddy to find some place to sleep.

That was where he was now. Lying in the dark on ten or so tumbling mats, Honey Bear cuddled up next to him. It was driving Teddy crazy to be this close, to touch Honey Bear and not have him. Even with this hot new body, Honey Bear only had eyes for Papa. If only Honey had eyes for him, so he could finally taste his sweetness.

Teddy untangled himself from Honey, the urgent need to empty his bladder and get more Build and Burn pressing on him. Plunging the needle into his skin, Teddy eyed the stack of vials, noting how many were missing. He looked at Honey, then glared angrily at the closed office door that Papa claimed as his own.

Teddy pulled the needle from his arm. *He's hoarding it for himself.* Dropping the needle in the trash bin, he headed for the locker room to relieve himself. *I'll show that bastard he can't hold out on us.* Teddy sighed at the release of the stream of hot piss. *I'll take Honey from him, then I'll take Build and Burn.*

After emptying his bladder, Teddy felt the need for release. His balls yearned to be emptied. After having seen the remains of Papa's first conquests, he knew someone not on Build and Burn was not an option. Honey didn't want him. Papa, whether he wanted Teddy or not, was definitely out of the question.

Washing his hands, Teddy looked at his reflection in the dirty mirror. He finally took a moment to really look at himself. He ran a hand over his stubbled jaw, taking in his roguish features. Teddy's dick began to stir. Without even thinking, his other hand found his pink round nipple.

Fuck, I'm hot. Teddy pushed his shorts down. He spat in his hand, then grabbed his rapidly filling self. *Who needs them when I can have sex with the sexiest man here? Me.* Teddy gripped his hard, thick meat. A throaty rumble came from Teddy's throat as his hand slowly pumped.

First, I'll take care of Papa. Teddy ran his palm over the head. *Then I'll break Honey Bear.* His hand moved down his shaft. *Then Build and Burn will be mine.* With his other hand, Teddy squeezed the nub of his nipple between his thumb and forefinger. *Then I'll destroy Diego Sanz for the fun of it.*

Teddy twisted his nipple harder. Pumping faster, Teddy watched himself in the mirror. He saw it, the hot and sexy beast of a man that he was—that would make all the men quiver with desire. They would all come flocking to him. Why wouldn't they? He was Teddy Bear, their heart's desire.

Licking his lips, he imagined himself surrounded by his harem of hot young men, all worshiping his body, vying for the privilege to taste his man meat. They would adorn his body with kisses, hoping to be chosen. Of course, none of them would be. None of them would be man enough to actually take him. They weren't worthy.

Teddy pumped harder. He could feel the surge building in his balls. He spread his trembling legs. Closing his eyes, he wasn't in front of a dirty mirror jerking off; he was surrounded by his worshipers, on their knees, mouths open, and eyes begging to be blessed with the taste of his essence.

Teeth gritted, body quaking, the sound of pleasure came from deep in Teddy's belly. He felt it creeping up from his balls. His hard-on throbbed in his tight grip. Like a busted fire hydrant, Teddy sprayed everywhere. His white residue was a sharp contrast to the yellowing porcelain sink as it dripped down.

In Teddy's mind, he was anointing his worshipers. They would be crawling over each other's naked bodies to catch his flying seed, trying to gorge themselves on his sacred seed.

Then, in a sexual frenzy, they'd start licking it off each other, fighting each other to fill their mouths with Teddy's juices.

Flicking his hand clean, Teddy opened his eyes, an insidious satisfactory grin on his face. *I'll play their game for now.* Teddy smiled at himself in the mirror. Turning on the water and washing his hands, Teddy began laughing quietly to himself. *Oh, the ways I could kill Papa Bear.*

CHAPTER 19

ALEX WOKE UP WITH THE BRIGHTEST SMILE on his face that faded when he realized he was alone in his bed. Falling asleep, curled up next to Shadow Guardian, had been even better than the night he'd been rescued. Waking up without him wouldn't have been so bad had he not remembered that Shadow Guardian said he wouldn't be back.

Alex hadn't wanted to get out of bed after that, and he didn't want to lie there being reminded that he was alone. *It is what it is,* he told himself, crawling out of bed and going about his day. *It was fun while it lasted.*

As the day drew on, he found himself looking forward to a visit that wasn't going to happen. He'd lost himself in the idea, not of dating Shadow Guardian, but of actually dating someone. He'd scold himself for such a foolish fantasy. Men didn't date guys like him. They only wanted one thing from him.

The last time he was on an app, some faceless profile had told him he was a bottomist and wanted to do a thorough and eight-inch-deep examination of Alex's bottom. What Alex assumed was the person's dick followed. Like the thirty times after he downloaded the app again, he swore he'd never go on there again and deleted the app.

Sitting on his couch, feeling lonely, Alex debated downloading the app again, stupidly expecting a different outcome. His finger was hovering over the download icon when he heard the sound of knuckles rapping on wood. For a moment, Alex was excited until he realized the sound was coming from his front door and not his bedroom.

Alex pushed himself off the couch, mentally kicking himself. "Coming. Who is it?" Alex peered through the peephole to see a ruggedly handsome, yet bruised, face.

"Strip-o-gram. I'm supposed to deliver my package here," the man cheerily announced loudly enough for his neighbors to hear.

Alex quickly yanked the door open. "Dude! I have neighbors!" Alex shouted.

"I know. Who do you think told me to do that?" The man grinned conspiratorially. Alex caught a giggling Ms. Jackson disappearing into the apartment behind the man. "I'm Freddy."

Alex stared at the man's outstretched hand a moment before it clicked who he was. "Esmeralda's cousin," Alex clarified, taking the man's hand. "Pleasure to meet you."

"And you're Alex. The one she asked to keep an eye on me." Releasing his hand, Freddy winked at Alex. "I hope you enjoy the view. Too bad I won't get to move in for a month or so. I wanted to give everyone my contact information and assure them that I'm here for them. That I'll take care of any issues they have."

Alex shifted awkwardly. "I'm sure everyone was relieved to hear that. I'm betting they were a little taken aback by those bruises. Did you recently have a match?"

"Yeah, I had a match last night." Freddy made a show of running his thumb over his busted lip and bruised cheek. "Esmerelda told you I was a boxer, apparently, but did she tell you I was an artist as well?"

"She did. She didn't say what type of artist, though." Alex had a playful, flirty air to his voice.

"Painting, drawing, and sculpting. I'm good with my hands." Freddy smirked.

"You'll have to show me sometime." Alex's eyes widened when he realized what he had said. "Your work, not that you're good with your hands. Not that I would mind finding out if you're good with your hands, but I'm kind of seeing someone, so I don't think it would be right, but we could be friends."

Freddy laughed, handing Alex his card. "You're cute. Give me a call. I'd love to hang out sometime." Freddy took a step back. "Feel free to look at my ass as I walk away." Freddy made a show of walking away. He turned just before going down the stairs to catch Alex watching. "See ya."

"Okay, boys," Papa growled, injecting himself with another dose of Build and Burn. "Dose up and get ready." He pulled the needle from his skin. "Let's go over the plan again."

"We know the fucking plan," Teddy groused, snatching his dose off the stack. "We put on the dumb bear masks, break into the warehouse with the chemicals we need, take what we need, and get the fuck out."

"Then we come back here and celebrate." Honey pressed his body to Papa. "You think we could, maybe, celebrate early?" Honey danced his fingers up Papa's chest.

Papa shoved Honey off him. "Get off me. Focus. We need to start making more Build and Burn and start finding people to test it on." Papa walked away. "Maybe we can find some that aren't big fuck ups like the two of you."

"Enjoy it while it lasts. I'll soon be the new Papa in this bear cave," Teddy said under his breath.

"What was that, Teddy? Did you have something to share?" Papa snarled.

Teddy recoiled. "Uh, no. I'm just worried about these shock sticks working."

Honey yawned. "Those are just backups. If you can't handle two security guards, then maybe you don't deserve Build and Burn anymore."

Teddy's nostrils flared with annoyance. Teddy bared his teeth at Honey. "I didn't say that. I said I was worried about these things malfunctioning, but I'm guessing you're okay with a hundred thousand volts going through you."

"Enough! Get your masks, get the shock sticks, and let's get going before I replace you both!" Papa commanded.

"You've been on patrol for three hours, and nothing has happened." Diego ignored Juan Carlos's chastising voice in his ear. "Why don't you just come home and get some sleep?" Diego stretched out his right hand and shot a shadow tendril out. "You can't ignore me all night."

Diego did a running jump off the building and swung himself over to the next building. "Will you talk to me already?" Diego deftly landed on the neighboring building. "You know I can remotely turn your suit off if I like." With the tendril returning to the suit, Diego went to the building edge and peered over, looking for any trouble. "Diego, talk to me."

Diego bit the inside of his cheek. "Just a while longer." Diego looked longingly toward Alex's building. "I need to clear my head." Diego reluctantly turned away. A red light began blinking in the corner of Diego's eye. "What is that?"

"An alarm at one of our warehouses." Diego didn't like the concern in Juan Carlos's voice. "It's where I stored the chemicals Dr. Wyatt ordered for that atrocity, Build and Burn."

"You don't think?" Diego's muscles tensed. When Juan Carlos didn't answer, he said, "I'm on it."

Diego drifted over the fence into the warehouse yard. As soon as his feet touched the ground, the glider wings melded back into his suit. With the gate wide open, Diego saw no sign of a break-in or of the guards. Something was definitely wrong here. He tapped his temple twice to activate the thermal imaging in his lenses.

Looking over at the guard trailer, he saw the forms of two men wiggling on the floor. "Looks like the guards are tied up in the trailer," Diego reported back to Juan Carlos. He turned his attention to the warehouse. "I can't see anything in the warehouse. Too much interference."

"Be careful," Juan Carlos warned. "I'm calling the police."

Diego cautiously moved toward the warehouse. "Wait. If it's Dr. Wyatt, maybe I can reason with him."

"If he could be reasoned with, he'd still be with the company." Juan Carlos let out an audible sigh, knowing Diego wouldn't listen. "Just be careful."

"I will." Diego crept along the edge of the building. He tapped his temple again, turning his vision normal. Diego peered around the corner at the loading bays. "There's three of them," Diego reported. "I don't think it's Dr. Wyatt."

"Why? Who else would want this stuff?" Juan Carlos asked.

"They're muscular, dressed in leather, and wearing bear masks." Diego double tapped his other temple. "Have a look."

"Diego, get out of there," Juan Carlos ordered. "Let's leave this one for the police."

"There's only three of them. I can take them," Diego argued. "Besides, we'd be lucky if the police showed up before sunrise. This is North Side." Diego turned the corner and started toward the truck being loaded. "I'm going in."

Diego moved stealthily forward. The man with the yellow accents came out and loaded the truck. When he went to return to the warehouse, he cocked his head and looked directly at Diego. Diego was spotted. The man pulled a small baton from his back and started toward Diego. He tapped a button, and the end of the baton sparked to life.

When they were almost within arm's reach, the masked man thrust the modified cattle prod at Diego. Diego deftly dodged it and swung out with his right hand. Landing the punch across the man's chin, Diego expected him to fall. Instead, he turned his head questioningly at Diego, then started laughing.

The masked man swung wildly at Diego, trying to land an electrified hit. Diego dodged, all the while landing kicks and blows that didn't seem to have any effect on the crazed man. The man in the yellow bear hood just laughed like it was a game while he continued swinging the baton wildly, trying to land an electrifying blow.

Changing his tactics, Diego grabbed him by the wrist, twisted the man's arm until he dropped the electric prod, and he had the man's arm behind his back. Diego kicked the back of the man's knee, causing him to drop to one knee. The man finally stopped laughing and howled in pain.

Diego was about to grab a zip tie from his suit when he felt strange. He wanted to let this man go and do whatever this man wanted to make him happy. Diego was vaguely aware of Juan

Carlos yelling through his earpiece when he let go of the man's arm and stepped back. Diego's head felt jumbled.

The man in the yellow bear hood stood and turned to face Diego. "Everyone wants Honey." Diego knew that voice. "Right, Teddy?"

Diego's head cocked to the side when a powerful blow came across his cheek. "Leave Honey alone!" Diego stumbled but caught himself. He saw a hulking man in a green bear hood looming, ready to attack. "Who is this creep?"

"I think they call him Shadow Guardian." Honey grabbed his electric prod off the ground. "Let's take him back with us so I can play with him some more."

Diego tried to shake the clouds from his head, but he grew angry. Angry because this Teddy was obviously familiar with Honey. He was preventing Diego from being near Honey. Diego launched himself at Teddy, intent on taking the bulky man down. When Diego collided with Teddy, the air was knocked out of his lungs.

Massive arms surrounded Diego. "I'm going to crush you. First, your bones will snap, then your organs will pop like squishy balloons." Diego tried to fight against the pressure of the arms trying to squeeze the life from him. "Then I'm going to stomp your lifeless body into the ground until there is nothing left to identify you."

"Save the suit. Papa will like how I look in it." Honey called out behind Diego.

Rage and desire clouded Diego's mind. He struggled futilely against Teddy's vice grip. He couldn't make out what Juan Carlos was screaming in his ear. All Diego wanted to do was destroy Teddy and keep Honey for himself. That was all that mattered—if he could just break free of Teddy's bear grip.

Diego jolted with electricity. Sparks of blue danced across his vision. The constricting force was suddenly gone, and Diego was sprawled out on the ground, breathing heavily. White and dark spots filled Diego's vision as he tried to recover. He could barely make out Teddy on the ground, groaning.

"I'm taking over," Juan Carlos announced through the ringing in Diego's ear. "I'm getting you out of there." Diego's head flew back from the kick from Honey's boot. "You'll pay for that. No one hurts my boy."

Diego's arm moved on its own, reaching out toward Honey. A tendril shot out from Diego's fingers and attached itself to Honey's body. A second later, Honey convulsed with the pulse of electricity Diego's suit pumped through his body. The tendril withdrew as Honey fell to the ground.

Diego's suit lifted his body to his feet. "I've got a car coming for you now. Just hold on tight," Juan Carlos announced in Diego's ear. Diego turned to look at the groaning bodies on the ground. "Your suit is almost out of power." Diego saw what he assumed to be Papa coming toward him. "You're leaving me no choice."

Diego's eyes grew heavy with sleep. "Don't," he managed to say before his suit turned him away from the rapidly approaching figure. He tried to fight the will of the suit. He was vaguely aware of his body being forced to run away before everything went dark.

CHAPTER 20

J UAN CARLOS WATCHED ESMERELDA EXAMINE
the slumbering, battered, and bruised Diego. With a nod,
she confirmed what the medical scanners had already told
Juan Carlos. With a gentle touch, she took Juan Carlos by the
elbow and guided him out to the living room. Leaving him on
the couch, she prepared them each a strong cup of coffee.

Setting the cup in front of Juan Carlos, Esmerelda went
for the jugular before sitting on the love seat. "What was he
thinking? What were you thinking?" Blowing on her coffee
before sipping, she added, "Okay, with that out of the way,
I've got a healing herb that will have him up in a day or so, but
he'll need to rest."

Juan Carlos put his head in his hands. "We both know he
won't do that."

With the air of a cold, calculating diva, Esmerelda crossed
her legs. "I'll put a little something in his food to make sure
he does. Now what the hell happened out there?"

Juan Carlos didn't answer right away, choosing to drink from his coffee to give himself a moment to contemplate the events that had occurred a short time ago. "We weren't prepared. We jumped into a situation we knew nothing about, and Diego almost lost his life. I should have had you and Freddy—"

"Freddy and I are not vigilante babysitters." The bite in Esmerelda's tone caused Juan Carlos to cringe. Softening her voice, she said, "Don't get me wrong: we appreciate what you and Diego have done for us, for our family, but you know we have our own demons to fight."

Juan Carlos used the last weapon in his arsenal. Guilt. "I know, but if this drug gets out, it's about protecting our community."

Esmerelda scoffed. "You haven't cared about our community since you stopped performing."

"That's a lie." It was a half-truth, and Juan Carlos knew it. It was a lie he told himself to justify his decisions. "I stopped performing to help Diego. I had to focus on him." Looking at Esmeralda, Juan Carlos knew he had to admit the truth. "You're right. Things are not going like we had hoped. Things are slipping through the cracks, and we've sacrificed promises we shouldn't have."

Esmeralda relaxed in the chair. "Now, what are you going to do about it?"

Juan Carlos chewed his bottom lip in contemplation. "We're going to make good on our promises." Juan Carlos reached over to put his hand on Esmerelda's knee. "I promise you: we'll find that cure for Federico."

Esmerelda patted his hand before covering it with her own. "Thank you, but we both know there's only one cure." Esmeralda sighed. "What do you need?"

Juan Carlos relaxed back onto the couch. "Thank you, but you don't…" Esmerelda held up a hand to let him know the matter was decided. "We need eyes and ears on the streets. We need to find these bears and rescue the men they kidnapped." Juan Carlos looked sheepishly at her. "I would like backup when we confront them, and if you could look at the drug they're making." Juan Carlos braced for the rebuke.

Esmerelda raised her mug to her lips, pinky extended. She took a long healthy sip before setting the cup down and making a show of brushing out the wrinkles of her skirt when she uncrossed her legs. "Okay." Juan Carlos almost jumped up to sing her praises, then she added, "But it comes with conditions."

Crossing his legs, Juan Carlos brought his cup to his lips, pinky extended. "Name them," he said coolly. She knew he wouldn't deny her anything reasonable.

"We only go in if we're needed, and Diego can't know about Freddy's illness or that we'll be there."

"Agreed."

"I want to use your garden."

Juan Carlos narrowed his eyes suspiciously. His garden was his sanctuary. "Why?"

"It's getting too hard to get the ingredients for Freddy's medicine." Esmerelda's voice cracked slightly with concern. "I almost didn't get him his medicine before he..." Her voice trailed off.

"Done." Juan Carlos's heart broke for them. He was one of the few that knew about their special bond that wasn't family. "You should have told me."

Esmerelda waved her hand dismissively. "I know, but it turned out okay, so let's move on." There was a wicked glint in Esmerelda's eyes that worried Juan Carlos. "I want Dolores Salvaje to perform at my fundraisers."

"Why?" came Juan Carlos's pointed response.

Esmerelda sipped her coffee, letting the silence between them linger. She saw it in his face, the *yes* that perched on the tip of his tongue, waiting for that gentle push. "Because you miss performing. I can see it every time I see you. You dress up your fancy suits, but I see Dolores Salvaje itching to get out. You keep stifling her, pretending she never existed. Why?"

The answer was one that Juan Carlos never shared with anyone. Not even Diego. "It's what's best for Diego and the business. It was hard enough being who we are trying to succeed, add in drag queen—"

"Fabulous and fierce drag queen," Esmerelda interjected.

"Fabulous and fierce drag queen," Juan Carlos repeated. "It just wasn't good for business."

Esmerelda scoffed. "Everyone but yours. And when was the last time you went out on a date?"

Juan Carlos sipped his coffee, letting the question hang between them. The negotiation had turned into one of their reality check conversations. Nothing was off limits here, and though feelings could be hurt, they always left these conversations for the better. "I could ask the same thing of you, or are you saving yourself for Gato?"

Esmerelda kept her tone flat and even when she answered, "Gato is in prison, and I have gone out trying to meet men. I just haven't found anyone—"

"That was Gato," Juan Carlos finished. Esmerelda glared at him. "I will revive Dolores Salvaje if you admit your true feelings for Gato."

They both sipped their coffee, eyes locked. Esmerelda was about to deny the accusation when Juan Carlos said, "He still asks about you." Esmerelda's hand trembled, the only sign in her stoic stature that it affected her. "I pulled some strings and got him moved to a better prison. I have a legal team working on getting his conviction overturned."

Esmerelda's eyes welled with tears. "Juan Carlos, don't. He nearly killed a man."

"To save you."

Esmerelda set her coffee down to keep her trembling hand from spilling it. "I know." She took a deep breath to calm her nerves. "Okay, yes, I have feelings for Gato. I always have. Are you happy now?"

Juan Carlos set his coffee down, then moved to kneel before Esmerelda. Holding her hands in his, he said, "I'll be happy when you're happy." Juan Carlos squeezed her hands. "Will you do me one last favor?"

Esmerelda laughed through her tears. "What?"

Juan Carlos brushed away a tear from her cheek. "Help me find myself again."

Esmerelda threw her head back in laughter. "Of course." She wiped away the tears. "Now that we've hashed all that out." An impish grin spread across her rosy cheeks. "I've got money that says Freddy kisses Alex before Diego."

Juan Carlos laughed. "Diego already kissed him as Shadow Guardian."

"That doesn't count."

"Okay, I'll take that bet." Returning to his seat, Juan Carlos smiled smugly. "I have faith in my boy."

"And I have faith in my cousin."

CHAPTER 21

DIEGO STRUGGLED TO OPEN HIS EYES. "Joder." He winced in pain. It took a moment for the sleep to clear his eyes so he could see Juan Carlos sitting in vigil beside his bed. "What happened? I feel like I got hit by a truck." Diego tried to sit up but fell back onto the pillow when a wave of pain shot through him. "Was I hit by a truck?"

"No," Juan Carlos answered somberly. "Your crazy Goldilocks ass tried to take on the three bears and lost." Juan Carlos put a hand on Diego's arm to keep him from getting up. "Voice analysis of the two you fought confirms it was Timmy and Jimmy. Which means..."

"Dr. Wyatt is probably the third," Diego finished. "They took Build and Burn." Juan Carlos nodded. Diego tried to get up again. "I need to get out there and stop them." Diego winced in pain. "Fuck!"

"You need to stay in bed and heal." Juan Carlos took a bottle of water from the nightstand and pressed it to Diego's lips. "Here. Drink." Diego took a swig from the bottle. "Besides, you can't go anywhere in the suit. It's still repairing itself, and I need to get some upgrades done before you tangle with them again."

"What upgrades?" Diego shifted carefully on the bed. "And what was that in the suit that made me pass out, and how did the suit move on its own?"

"I had a built-in safety protocol installed that let me remotely take control of the suit and incapacitate you if need be." Juan Carlos rolled his eyes at Diego's scowl. "Don't look at me like. It saved your life. Honey was emitting some powerful pheromones, and it was clouding your judgment."

"I want that removed from the suit. I can't have you sec-ond-guessing me out there," Diego barked.

Juan Carlos folded his arms across his chest defiantly. "I will not. That protocol saved your ass last night, and you won't be going out again until we get the suit upgraded with air fil-ters and something that can take those bears down."

"They use tranquilizer darts in shows," Diego joked. "Or maybe we can lure them into a trap with picnic baskets."

Juan Carlos stood. "Not funny, Diego. I need to get to the office and handle this. I asked Esmerelda to watch over you. Do what she says." Juan Carlos lowered his voice. "I told her the rope broke while climbing your rock wall."

Diego groaned. "No, not her. She'll make me drink one of her potions. You know she's a witch."

"Gitana," Esmeralda corrected from the doorway. "And the only potion that I brought is my puchero." She nodded to Juan Carlos. "Go. I got this."

"Gracias, mi vida." Juan Carlos pecked Esmerelda on the cheek. "Feel free to smack him if he misbehaves." Juan Carlos paused a moment before leaving. "Save me some puchero?"

Esmerelda smiled devilishly. "Of course. Now go. I have an ungrateful patient to tend to. Don't be surprised if he has a tail when you get back."

An hour later, Juan Carlos sat in his office with Detective Aaron Heath on the other side of his desk. Dion had put him off for as long as possible, but the distinguished man with silver streaks in his chestnut hair wanted answers that Juan Carlos had but couldn't give truthful answers to. At least not the full truth.

"You're being very elusive, Mr. Sanz. Need I remind you that two men are missing?" Detective Heath commented after another of Juan Carlos's vague answers.

Juan Carlos sighed. "I know. The warehouse that was broken into houses the projects that are earmarked too dangerous or failures." Juan Carlos mentally debated revealing the next bit of information before he did. "We recently let go of one of our scientists, Dr. Wyatt. He was trying to develop a drug that helped fight obesity, but it had horrific side effects, not to mention the ethical issues."

Juan Carlos picked up his tablet and brought up the pictures of Dr. Wyatt, Timmy, and Jimmy. "We believe that Dr. Wyatt and his lab assistants took the experimental drug and broke into the warehouse." Juan Carlos passed the tablet to Detective Heath. "We believe their motive was to get the last of the chemicals we had stored for the scrapped drug before it was repurposed or destroyed."

"These don't look like the type of guys who could pull this off, and why would they kidnap the two security guards?" Detective Heath handed back the tablet.

"New test subjects." Juan Carlos brought up the pictures of Honey, Teddy, and Papa from Shadow Guardian's suit. "This is what we believe they look like now." Juan Carlos handed the tablet back. "Based on what they are wearing, we believe that they were responsible for the fire at the leather shop and that they may have kidnapped the owner."

"That's a big leap, but since we can't locate the owner or a motive..." Detective Heath said solemnly. "I shouldn't be telling you this, but three other men have been reported missing." Detective Heath studied the images. "If the drug had this type of result, why was it scrapped?"

"We wanted something to help with weight loss." Juan Carlos motioned with his arm, disgusted. "That. That is an abomination. It has a high mortality rate. Anyone who uses it and survives becomes addicted to it while their organs fail. Now we can assume there are mental side effects."

"I'll need copies of these photos and their home addresses if you have them. How did you get those photos, by the way?" Detective Heath handed back the tablet.

"Drone," Juan Carlos lied coolly. "They destroyed it before I could maneuver it out of there."

"Drone," Detective Heath repeated suspiciously. He pulled out his phone and looked at the screen. "Did they take anything else that you know of?"

"We'll have to do an inventory, but I'll—" Juan Carlos stopped mid-thought. "Is something wrong?"

"I'm sorry. I think we just found those three missing men, or rather, their bodies." Detective Heath put away his phone. "Do you have a way to test for the drug?"

"No, but it wouldn't be hard to test for it. We would just need a blood or tissue sample." Juan Carlos said a silent prayer for the three men. "Whatever you need, DJC is at your disposal."

"Thank you. If you think of anything, please, reach out to me." Detective Heath scribbled on his notepad then, tore the paper off. "Here." He handed the paper over to Juan Carlos. "That has all my contact information." He winked at Juan Carlos. "Including my personal cell, in case you want to use it."

Flustered, Juan Carlos took the paper and stood when Detective Heath did. "Yes, um, of course." Juan Carlos remembered himself for a moment. "I already had my assistant Dion pull the information you needed." Juan Carlos ran his fingers over the stack of Post-It notes on his desk. Growing bold, he snatched a pen off his desk and scribbled his information down. "My contact information, in case you need anything from me." Juan Carlos handed over the tiny slip of paper.

"Thank you." Detective Heath gave Juan Carlos a soft smile. "I'll be in touch."

Juan Carlos watched with bated breath as the muscular body of the detective left. Once the door shut, he fell back into his chair, doing his best not to swoon like a lovesick teenager. When his door opened again, Juan Carlos quickly straightened, thinking it was the detective returning.

"Do you need anything?" Dion asked, the hint of a rare smile on her lips. "Coffee? Tea? Cold shower?" She stifled a giggle at Juan Carlos's glare. "Alex asked you to come see him in his office."

"Tell him I'll be there shortly." Juan Carlos put on his professional tone. "Oh, and Dion, not a word to Diego." She put two fingers to her lips and made like to zip them. "I'm glad we understand each other." Juan Carlos relaxed. "He was hot, wasn't he?"

"If I were into men, I'd do him," Dion answered. "Go get 'em, boss."

CHAPTER 22

A LEX HAD BEEN BUSY MOST OF THE MORNING
working on the special project Juan Carlos had waiting
for him when he got in that morning. Juan Carlos had emailed
him instructions that he wanted to boost the power and add
an air filtration system to an experimental hazmat suit. Alex
thought they were simple requests until he opened the files.

As he sifted through the data, Alex realized this wasn't just
some ordinary hazmat suit. Needing to understand what he
was looking at better, he created a computerized model of the
suit. When the image came up, Alex was certain that he had
unconsciously altered the data. He knew that figure all too well.

Alex studied the screen before double-checking the
inputted data. "What in the world? This can be right." Alex ran
his fingers over the familiar image. "That's Shadow Guardian."

Alex pondered what he was seeing for a moment. He
brought up his email and was about to shoot Juan Carlos a
message when he stopped himself. "Digital trail," he said to
himself. Foolish or not, Alex wondered if Juan Carlos was

Shadow Guardian. He could be secretly working on the suit of the man that rescued him.

He picked up his office phone and buzzed Dion to see if Juan Carlos was free, only to be told he was in an important meeting. "Can you have him come see me as soon as he can?" Alex asked Dion. "It's about the special project he sent me."

Hanging up with Dion, he started working on what Juan Carlos asked of him. He toyed with the simulation, changing variables, adding the features Juan Carlos wanted, and watched the suit system crash and kill the virtual body inside either by suffocating them when the breathing system failed or electrocuting them when the inevitable charge in the batteries released.

What am I missing? Alex stood and paced about the room. He stopped and looked up at the imposing image of the suit he had on the big screen. *They obviously figured out a way to charge you. Why can't I supercharge you?* Something clicked in Alex's head. *Charge. You don't need more power; you need to charge faster.*

Alex rushed back to his seat and began typing away until he found the right specifications and code. "Okay." Alex began studying how the suit charged itself. "The suit recharges itself using the motion of the person wearing it," he said aloud. "What if we improve that efficiency?"

Alex changed some of the code, then uploaded it to the simulation. According to Juan Carlos's email, it was for a defibrillator function in the suit, but that didn't seem right for a hazmat suit. He watched as the virtual suit discharged its stored energy to minimal levels, then did jumping jacks to recharge itself rapidly, then discharged another burst.

"It worked." Alex felt a surge of pride, then laughed at the image, seeing Shadow Guardian on the screen instead of the digital model. "Okay, one problem solved. Now the next one."

The next solution came to Alex ten minutes before Juan Carlos came into his office. He studied how the suit's breathing system worked. It was similar to how lungs worked, exchanging the outside air with the inside air. Juan Carlos wanted a filter without adding any unnecessary bulk to the suit. Alex couldn't think of anything when inspiration hit him from the most unlikely of places.

"You wanted to see me?" Juan Carlos entered to see Alex standing in front of the big screen on the wall, watching a digitized version of Diego's suit doing jumping jacks and shooting sparks from its hands. "Are you playing a video game?"

Alex beamed proudly when he turned around. "No. I wasn't able to do exactly what you wanted, but I did the next best thing. Come see." Alex studied Juan Carlos as he moved. *The body is all off. It can't be Juan Carlos.*

Juan Carlos studied the screen. "Why is he doing jumping jacks? What are all those random dots around him?"

Alex turned his attention back to the screen. "Okay, so you wanted to give the batteries more storage capacity, but every time I did that, I fried the wearer," Alex explained. "Instead, I found a way to optimize the recharging of the batteries. See?" Alex indicated the charge levels on the side of the screen. "After every electrical discharge, it takes just a few jumping jacks, and the suit is fully recharged again."

"Interesting." Juan Carlos grinned at the thought of Diego randomly doing jumping jacks to recharge his suit. "Theoretically, any movement could recharge it just as fast. It doesn't necessarily have to be jumping jacks, does it?"

"Correct." Alex took a risk with his next question. "Why would a hazmat suit need a defibrillator function, though?"

"Special request from the client," Juan Carlos answered without missing a beat. "What about the air filters?"

"That's those little dots," Alex continued, not missing how Juan Carlos answered the question without actually answering it. Alex motioned to the other side of the screen. "Those represent various sizes of air particles. As you can see from the simulation, the filters I designed keep almost one hundred percent of the particles out."

"Interesting." Juan Carlos studied the numbers. "What type of filtering process are you using?"

"I actually had to redesign the airflow of the suit. It was great and everything, but for what you wanted, not so much." Alex tapped on the monitor to bring up just the breathing system. "The suit still uses the outside air to cool itself down, but the air that goes to the wearer only comes from here." The screen zoomed in on the neck.

Juan Carlos leaned forward to study the image closer. "What are those? Are those gills?"

"Sort of." Alex fidgeted, not sure how well Juan Carlos was liking what he had come up with. "I based them off of gills. It was impossible to filter all the air for the suit without the system completely overloading and shutting down, but these special gills, for lack of a better word, have a sole purpose of supplying air."

Alex waited nervously as Juan Carlos tapped the screen and changed the angle. "Interesting." Juan Carlos straightened and clasped his hands behind his back. "How did you come up with this idea?"

Alex began chuckling. "You're going to laugh. I was thinking about having fish for lunch." Juan Carlos looked at him in disbelief, and Alex felt the need to explain further. "You know, I was hungry, and thought about having fish. Then I was like, you know fish filter oxygen from the water with their gills. Which led to me wondering what it would be like if we had gills, and..."

"Stop," Juan Carlos interrupted. "You were inspired by fish, to put it simply."

Alex scratched at the back of his head, embarrassed. "Yeah, I sometimes ramble."

Juan Carlos gave Alex a warm smile. "I've noticed, and no offense, but sometimes your train of thought is too long of a ride for a distinguished man like me."

Alex shrugged. "I get it. I get excited when someone asks me how I came up with an idea, and then I start telling them. Before I know it, they are looking at me like I'm crazy, and I have this need to show them I'm not, so I continue on, and on and on. Then it's like an hour later, and they are still looking at me like I'm crazy..."

"Alex!" Juan Carlos interrupted. "I don't think you're crazy, but from now on, can I take the express train?"

"Sure. I'll do my best. Maybe I can..." Alex trailed off when he saw the look Juan Carlos gave him. "Express train. Right."

"There's one more thing the client wants to include in the suit." Juan Carlos turned his attention back to the screen. "Tranquilizer darts. Strong enough to take down a bear."

"Tranquilizer darts? Why on earth would they need tranquilizer darts?" Alex questioned.

"It's what the client wants." Juan Carlos shrugged, again answering without an answer. "Be glad I said no to the picnic basket."

"Picnic basket?" Alex repeated, not understanding. "What good would a picnic basket do?"

"Your guess is as good as mine." Juan Carlos shook his head. "I'm told bears like them."

"Bears?" Alex questioned. "I thought this was a hazmat suit? When did bears get involved in this?"

"I'm not really sure. Well, why don't you have your lunch? I need to go check up on Diego. He had a little fall." Juan Carlos adjusted his clothing.

"Is he okay? What happened?" Alex asked with genuine concern.

"He was climbing a rock wall, and the rope snapped," Juan Carlos lied easily. "He's at home being tended to by Esmerelda. I need to make sure they haven't killed each other." Juan Carlos started to leave but turned to face Alex again. "Good work, by the way. Send me those specifications, and I'll put them through testing."

Alex watched Juan Carlos shut the door behind him, then mouthed the word, "Bears?"

CHAPTER 23

"**E**XACTLY WHAT ARE WE GOING TO DO WITH those two we have tied up in the locker room?" Teddy asked, injecting another dose of Build and Burn into his arm. "We don't have enough Build and Burn for them, too."

Papa sighed at the feeling of fresh Build and Burn flowing through his system. "We will. When Honey gets back, you and he will start making more."

Teddy tried to stifle his anger toward Papa. "Then what? What's our goal here?"

There was a maniacal tone to Papa's words. "We're going to build an army. Then we're going to destroy Diego Sanz and his company. Then I will rule Morgan City with an iron fist."

"We're going to need a bigger place," Teddy mumbled, turning away so Papa wouldn't see him roll his eyes. "The fool has no clue what he's doing."

"What was that? Did you have something to say?" Papa snarled, narrowing his eyes at Teddy.

Teddy turned around, baring his teeth in his best approximation of a smile. "I was just saying to myself that I should check in on the test subjects."

Papa worked his jaw, biting back harsh words. "You do that. Then get to work on Build and Burn."

"Yes, sir," Teddy said through gritted teeth. "Don't forget to check in on your little leather pet. He's starting to smell."

Teddy left before the urge to maul Papa took over. *When the time is right.* He entered the locker room. *I'll show him who the real daddy bear is.*

Teddy eyed the two men lying on the floor in their underwear. They were shackled to a bench bolted to the floor. *What is he going to be? A polar bear?* Teddy pondered, taking in the older man's silver-gray hair, bushy mustache, and ample belly. *He'd be good as a foot soldier, if that.*

Now that one. Teddy smiled, enjoying the sight of the tall, muscular cub with his short curly blond hair and wisps of chest hair poking out of his undershirt. *That one is sweet as sugar.* Teddy grinned. *He'd be my sugar bear.*

The older man sat up. "What are you looking at? Fucking perverted freaks. Do you like looking at me in my tightie-whities?"

The younger man rolled over onto his side. "Don't antagonize him. What are you going to do with us?"

Teddy only addressed the younger man. "For now, nothing. I just came in to check in on you, see if you need anything."

"Our clothes. Our freedom. Can you get us those things, motherfucker?" the older man spat out venomously.

Teddy's nostrils flared. "Keep it up, old man. I'll yank out your teeth so you'll be a gummy bear." Teddy ignored the perplexed look he got. His demeanor softened when he addressed the young man. "What about you? Do you need anything?"

"Will you at least let Phil go? You can keep me, but he's got a family," the young man pleaded.

"Then Papa will use the Build and Burn on you first," Teddy said, as if it should have been obvious to the men. "I won't have time to perfect it, to make sure it doesn't kill you."

The old man panicked. "You're going to kill us? I bet they want to fuck our dead bodies, then eat them."

"Phil, you're not helping. He can help us get out of here if he wants to," the young man scolded his friend. The young man sat up and looked at Teddy with imploring eyes. "Will you help us get out of here?"

"Then you wouldn't be here. I like you here," Teddy explained.

Phil groaned. "Stop talking to him, Joshua. Can't you see he's a lunatic like the other two?"

"I'd come back," Joshua pressed, ignoring his partner. "To visit. Maybe we could go out somewhere, for coffee or something."

Teddy's brow furrowed in contemplation. *If they aren't here, then Papa won't use Build and Burn on them.* He chewed on his lower lip, mentally debating. *Then I can perfect it before giving it to my Sugar bear. Then I can be with my Sugar.*

Teddy was about to agree when he heard Papa summoning him. "I need to go." Teddy shook away the rogue thoughts. "I'll bring you something to eat and drink." He bared his teeth at Phil. "For both of you."

Teddy left, hesitant to leave the sugary sweet cub. In the main room, he found Papa and Honey sitting on weight benches with a makeshift table of floor mats between them. They were busy shoving food into their mouths while Papa's little pet hungrily scarfed down what food he was given.

"Where did you get the money for all this? Couldn't you get something green or some sort of vegetable?" Teddy questioned, looking in one of the boxes filled with limp French fries, greasy burgers, and chicken sandwiches.

"I didn't have to pay. I just asked them to give it to me, and they did," Honey said with his mouth full of food.

"At least one of you two is able to do something right. What do we need vegetables for? We have Build and Burn." Papa inhaled more food.

"Next time, get me something healthy. I guess I'll feed your lab rats in the back." Teddy pulled the food from one of the boxes until there was enough for the two prisoners. Teddy's stomach rumbled audibly. He looked at the food, then to the door of the locker room. He snatched a burger and devoured it, satiating his craving.

"Go on. Go fatten them up so we can slim them down." Papa laughed through a mouth full of food.

Teddy ignored the comment as he strode back. He couldn't believe Honey, of all people, wouldn't have been sensitive to Teddy's issues with food. "Just because we have Build and Burn doesn't mean I want to clog my arteries," Teddy mumbled. "I don't want to end up back where I was." Teddy turned back to eye the two at their trough. *Why couldn't I be toned like Honey or muscled like Papa?*

CHAPTER 24

DIEGO STIRRED AT THE SOUND OF VOICES over him. Running his tongue over his dry lips, he opened his eyes to see Juan Carlos and Esmerelda talking in hushed tones. He stretched and yawned, feeling oddly fresh, but still sore. They stared at him with concern as he sat up in the bed.

Diego yawned. "What's going on? How long have I been out?" He scowled at Esmeralda. "She drugged me, didn't she?" He pointed an accusatory finger at her. "What did you do to me, witch?"

"Gitana. Respect her culture and heritage," Juan Carlos corrected, reaching out and lowering Diego's hand.

Esmeralda crossed her arms across her chest as she glared at Diego. "Thank you. You would think he would be nicer to me in case he grows a tail from the potion I gave him."

"She's kidding, right?" Diego looked at Juan Carlos, who just shrugged. "Tell me you're kidding."

"I'm kidding, quierdo. All I did was give you some healing herbs." Esmerelda reached out and stroked Diego's stubbly chin. "You fell asleep on your own. Your body needed rest."

"He pushes himself too hard. I keep telling him to slow down," Juan Carlos added.

"Like you're one to talk." Turning her attention to Juan Carlos, Esmeralda put her hands on her hips. "You're no better. If you're not at work, you're locked away in here. When was the last time you went out, let alone went on a date?"

"Yeah," Diego chimed in, then recoiled when he saw the look Esmeralda gave him.

Esmerelda pursed her lips. "Shall we talk about your love life? Or lack thereof?"

"Esmerelda, thank you so much for helping us today." Juan Carlos put a hand on Esmeralda's shoulder and began guiding her out of the room. "I am sure you're anxious to get home. Didn't Freddy have a match recently? Shouldn't you be checking up on him?"

"I should, but don't think this lets you off the hook about having a life." Esmerelda shot a look back at Diego. "Both of you."

Diego took advantage of the momentary privacy to get out of bed and find a pair of sleep pants to slip into. He twisted and stretched his body, noticing the pain had dulled itself to something he could manage. A couple of aspirin was all he needed, and he'd be able to head out tonight.

"Don't even think about heading out tonight." Juan Carlos's voice startled Diego. "Besides, the suit is still being repaired and upgraded."

Diego turned to see Juan Carlos's disapproving look. "Upgraded? You mean you're getting rid of those overrides you installed without my permission?"

Juan Carlos sat on the edge of the bed. He patted the space beside him. "No. I know you don't like them, but if I hadn't done what I did, you wouldn't be here to bitch about them," Juan Carlos explained. Diego, sulking, sat up in the bed. "In all the time you've worn the suit, have I ever overridden you?"

"No," Diego admitted reluctantly, "but..."

"No buts," Juan Carlos cut him off. "You may not be my son by blood, but you're my son by love. I'm going to do everything in my power to protect you. If you don't like it, I'll have the suit destroyed, and we'll be done with it all."

"I like butts, though," Diego joked, trying to lighten the mood. "Okay, leave the failsafe in. What are these upgrades?"

Diego listened to how Alex had improved his suit, his design, in ways that he hadn't even thought of. Diego wanted to jump up and rush to the lab to see them for himself, but he stayed put. He knew he wouldn't be able to resist trying them out before the suit was ready. He felt like a kid waiting for Christmas morning.

"What? No picnic basket?" Diego asked, deadpan.

"Put a shirt on, and let's eat dinner." Juan Carlos patted Diego's leg, then stood. "I'll tell you the rest after dinner."

After dinner, Diego relaxed on the sofa with Juan Carlos. As much as he wanted to head out into the night and find Dr. Wyatt and his minions, taking a night off to spend time with Juan Carlos and let his body rest was something he needed. Not that he'd admit it to Juan Carlos. If he did, Juan Carlos would make him take more time off the streets.

"Esmerelda really can cook for a witch." Diego rubbed his stomach.

"Gitana," Juan Carlos corrected. "Keep calling her a witch; see what happens."

"Gitana," Diego corrected himself. "Alright, tell me this news you've been putting off telling me. I know it's bad, so just go ahead and tell me already."

"Do you want coffee? I could use a cup of coffee. Let me make a pot." Diego's hand on Juan Carlos's leg stopped him from rising. "Fine." Juan Carlos settled back down on the sofa. "Dr. Wyatt and his crew have done more than just steal the chemicals for Build and Burn."

Juan Carlos took a deep breath, then made a sign of the cross. "I told Detective Aaron about our suspicions about Dr. Wyatt. They went to his house." Juan Carlos took a moment. "They found blood. Blood they believe to be a match to the three mutilated bodies they found in the landfill."

Juan Carlos put an arm out to keep Diego from bolting off the sofa. "There's more, and remember that your suit is still being repaired and upgraded, so there's nothing you can do tonight." Juan Carlos waited until Diego settled back down. "They also kidnapped the two security guards from the warehouse, possibly as test subjects."

"What?!" Diego exclaimed. "You should have told me! You should have held off on the upgrades until we got them back!" Diego jumped up and started pacing. "How could you keep this from me? You should have told me!"

"Sit your ass down. Now." Diego did, hearing the controlled anger behind Juan Carlos's voice. "I didn't tell you earlier because you needed to heal, your suit needed to repair itself, and you needed those upgrades." Juan Carlos put up a finger to silence Diego before he could speak. "If I had told you sooner, you'd have tried to go off half-cocked, and I would have had to drug you so you didn't get yourself killed."

Diego slumped in his seat, knowing Juan Carlos was right. "I'm sorry." Diego hugged Juan Carlos. "I shouldn't have yelled at you. You were right ... *are* right about me and the suit."

Juan Carlos hugged him back. "You're forgiven. As much as I hate to admit it, you're the best chance of bringing Dr. Wyatt, Timmy, and Jimmy to justice."

CHAPTER 25

ALEX STOOD IN THE DOORWAY OF HIS BED-room, looking at the window Shadow Guardian used. He wondered if he'd ever see Shadow Guardian again. That chance meeting, as terrifying as it was, was the start of everything changing for the better for him and those around him. It may have been a coincidence, but there was no denying that it was the first domino to fall.

Juan Carlos noticed him and gave him his dream job. He was able to pay off a big portion of his debt. The building was getting much-needed attention. Pat, if only temporarily, was off the streets. Just about everything in his life was getting better. Everything except his love life. That was still nonexistent.

Alex looked at the bed and remembered falling asleep curled up against Shadow Guardian. *Why did I think I could have someone as hot as him?* Alex stepped back into his living room. *He did kiss me, though.* Alex remembered the soft touch of Shadow Guardian's lips and the roughness of stubble.

Maybe I was just something to pass the time. Alex moved on to the kitchen, needing something cold to drink. *It wouldn't be the first time a guy ghosted me.* With his hand on the refrigerator handle, he paused, noticing Freddy's card. "No."

Alex yanked open the door and pulled out a water. Shutting the door, he cracked open the water and took a swig. "No," he said to the card screaming at him. "It wouldn't be a good idea." Alex pulled the card from the refrigerator. "He probably doesn't even remember who I am."

Moving back to the couch, Alex fingered the card. Sitting down, he stared at the card as if it would tell him what to do. Somehow it felt wrong, like he was betraying Shadow Guardian. The truth was, he felt like he was betraying his heart, as foolish as it might sound. He thought he had a connection with Shadow Guardian, but that was gone now.

"Screw it." Alex pulled out his phone and opened the messaging app. He was typing Freddy's number when he heard Juan Carlos's voice in his head telling him that texting was impersonal, that he should call. "Ugh, Juan Carlos. You and your old-fashioned ways."

Alex punched in the number, then stared at it, petrified at the thought of actually calling Freddy. What if he answered? What would he say to him? Worse, what if he got Freddy's voicemail and he did his verbal train wreck? He'd have to move or suffer the lethal embarrassment of seeing Freddy in his building.

"Fuck. Voicemail." Alex mentally cursed when the digital voice came on after two rings. Alex took a deep breath, hoping to be told the mailbox was full. The beep came, and the silence demanded to be filled.

"Hey, Freddy, this is Alex from the building. You were my strip-o-gram." Alex paused, closed his eyes, and reset himself. "I just wanted to know if you'd like to hang out. Call me."

CHAPTER 26

TEDDY SHACKLED PHIL BACK TO THE BENCH before nervously freeing Sugar. "Don't try anything. Otherwise, I won't be able to let you shower again," he said in a shaky voice.

"Okay." Joshua stood up, his hands still chained together. "I guess you can't free my hands."

"No," Teddy answered with disappointment. "Come on." Teddy motioned toward the showers, careful not to touch his Sugar. "Be glad you get to wash, unlike that poor creature in the main gym that sits in his own filth."

"Why are you doing this? You're not like them. Are you?" Joshua asked, grateful to be able to move his legs.

"I am," Teddy lied. "I took the Build and Burn just like them." Joshua stepped into the first stall. "I'll close the curtain; then, you can hand me your underwear."

"You don't want to see me naked? I don't mind you looking," Joshua said, putting a bit of devilishness in his voice.

"I do." Teddy closed the curtain, protecting himself from the temptation. "If I see you naked, I may not be able to control myself," he confessed. "You make me feel like I did for Honey," Teddy paused, feeling the pain of his words. "Before he took Build and Burn."

"You liked Honey?" Joshua's chained hand came out of the curtain, holding his underwear. "What happened?"

"Build and Burn." Teddy snatched the boxer briefs. He fought the urge to bring them to his nose and inhale. "He likes Papa. When he took the Build and Burn, he became pretty enough for Papa." Teddy heard the water cut on. "Too pretty for me."

"His loss," Joshua said over the sound of falling water. "You're not like them. I could tell when he, Papa, was it? When Papa told you to tie us up." Teddy heard the splatter of water hitting the floor. He imagined the water cascading over Joshua's body. "You hesitated. You didn't want to do it or to take us when you guys left."

Teddy fisted the underwear in his hand, running his fingers over the fabric. "You say you're like them, but you're not." Teddy wanted to tell his Sugar he was wrong, but he wasn't. "You're sweet and nice. They aren't." Joshua turned the water off. "Towel?"

Teddy stared at the wet hand coming out of the curtain for a moment. "Oh, yeah." He handed one of the musty gym towels over. "Honey was nice before he took Build and Burn. He was my friend. Not anymore. Not since he became Honey."

"Underwear." Joshua thrust the towel through the curtain. Teddy took it but found he didn't want to hand over the underwear. "Underwear?" Teddy handed over the boxer briefs. "How does that Build and Burn work?"

"It turns fat into muscle." The curtain opened, revealing a slightly wet Joshua. Teddy let out a belly growl. "Once you take it, you have to keep taking it."

"Isn't the brain like sixty percent fat?" Joshua stepped into Teddy's personal space. "How does it affect that?"

"I, uh." Teddy stepped back, needing the space between him and his Sugar. "I don't know."

"Maybe you should find out." Joshua stepped closer to Teddy. "Maybe you should stop taking it till you do."

Teddy said firmly. "No. I should kill Papa and fix it." Teddy noticed how close his Sugar was and moved away. "I can do it. I know I can."

"Don't try to kill him. You're a sweet Teddy Bear. Just set me and Phil free. Then turn yourselves into cops," Joshua pleaded.

"No," Teddy said vehemently. "If I set Sugar free, I'll never see Sugar again. I'll never get to taste Sugar."

"You will. I'll find you." Joshua inched forward cautiously, careful not to startle Teddy.

"No! You're trying to confuse me!" Teddy roared. Teddy gripped the sides of his head in pain. "Thinking hurts! Stop making me think!"

Joshua put his hands up in supplication and slowly backed. "I'm sorry. I didn't mean to. How about you just take me back to Phil?"

"Stop telling me what to do!" Teddy's eyes went wild and his nostrils flared. He swung his fist out, narrowly missing Joshua, hitting the wall and causing the tile to crack and break around his clenched hand. "No one tells Teddy what to do! Not anymore!"

"Okay, okay," Joshua said in a soothing voice, taking another step back. "What do you want to do? Take me back to Phil?"

Teddy glared at Joshua, seeing the fear he was causing the man. Teddy closed his eyes, anger turning into shame. "I, uh,

I want to take you back to the grumpy one." Teddy opened his eyes. "Come on."

Joshua put his hands down. "Okay. Anything else you want to do, like, maybe let Grumpy go so we can be alone?"

"I could kill him. That way, we can be alone, and Papa won't be that mad." Teddy bared his teeth at Joshua.

"No, don't do that," Joshua blurted out. "Sugar can't be with someone who kills," Joshua said, using the affectionate nickname for leverage. "You want to be with Sugar, right?"

Teddy covered his teeth with his lips. "Yes." Joshua saw Teddy mentally connecting the dots. "No Sugar if I kill. No kill, and I get Sugar?"

"Right." Joshua gave him a relaxed smile. "Sugar wants to be with you, but only if you don't kill." Teddy nodded in understanding. "Do you think you can remember that?"

"Yes, Teddy won't kill, but Teddy is in charge," Teddy said, chest heaving.

Joshua relaxed. "Yes, sir. Teddy is in charge. Teddy will protect Sugar, right? He won't let anything happen to Sugar or Grumpy. Right?"

Teddy sneered. "I don't like Grumpy. I'll protect Sugar and make sure nothing happens to Sugar."

"And Grumpy. You can't let anything happen to Grumpy, either," Joshua reiterated.

Teddy scrunched up his face in annoyance. "Fine. I won't let anything happen to Grumpy, either."

"Thank you." Joshua made to take a step forward but stopped when he saw Teddy tense again. "You're a good guy, Teddy. You shouldn't be hanging around with those other two."

"They are my..." Teddy struggled to describe Papa and Honey. Papa was never his friend, and Honey no longer was. "They are part of my den."

"You could make a new den with me," Joshua said sweetly. "Just stop taking that Build and Burn. Then we can go and make that den together, okay?"

"I can't. I'm addicted." Teddy looked shamefully at the floor.

"Maybe you could, I don't know," Joshua stepped closer to Teddy, "get addicted to Sugar?" Teddy looked up and smiled. "Maybe you can sneak me out for a date or something?"

Teddy scowled. "No. Sugar stays here where I can protect Sugar."

"Okay, okay. How about we just work on you getting off Build and Burn?" Joshua backed off.

Teddy shook his head angrily. "No. There's no getting off Build and Burn." Teddy scrunched his face, deep in thought. "Maybe, maybe I could fix it."

"That could work. Can I help?" Joshua stepped closer to Teddy. "You'd just have to free my hands and legs."

"No! You'll run away!" Teddy growled. Teddy narrowed his eyes at Joshua. "You're trying to trick me."

"No, no. I just want to help you. I want us to be together. Really." Joshua tried to keep his voice calm and even.

"Enough talking. You're making Teddy's brain hurt," Teddy huffed.

"Okay, okay." Joshua swallowed down his fear. "Take me back to Grumpy, and we'll talk again later, okay?"

"You talk too much," Teddy grumbled, turning to leave the showers. "Wish I could put my dick in your mouth to keep you from talking so much."

"Get off the Build and Burn, and you can. Maybe I'll let you do a little more," Joshua teased. Teddy stopped and glanced back at Joshua. Joshua saw the scowl turn into a slight smile. "We can talk about that later, too."

CHAPTER 27

"**E**SMERELDA, PLEASE TELL ME YOU HAVE good news." Juan Carlos greeted her with a hug and kiss on both cheeks.

Returning the gesture, she said, "I wish. Freddy is still out there sniffing around. It would help if we knew where to look."

Juan Carlos motioned toward the chair Detective Heath had occupied earlier. "Sit. You must be exhausted. Can I get you anything?"

"I'm good, thank you," she said, taking the seat. Juan Carlos didn't see the smug smile on her face until he took his seat. With anyone else, Juan Carlos would have played dumb, but he knew better than to do that with Esmerelda. "Call him. He likes you. He's a good man. Just what you need."

"How extensive are your abilities?" Juan Carlos caught movement in her eyes. He leaned forward to see green swirls in her golden, amber eyes. "Your eyes."

Esmeralda blinked rapidly, banishing the color from her pupils. She lowered her gaze so that she was still looking at

Juan Carlos but not meeting his eyes. "They've grown significantly." Meeting Juan Carlos's gaze again, she let out a soft laugh. "That wasn't from my powers, though. Dion told me before I came in. Oh, don't look at me like that. You'll get frown lines."

Juan Carlos's lips curled up into a smile. "You're a bitch; you know that."

"So are you," Esmerelda countered. She pulled a small bottle of pills from her clutch and set them on the desk. "Now, let's get down to why I'm here. I've tried, but I have nothing that can counteract this."

"Damn, none of our scientists have anything, either." Juan Carlos shook his head in dismay. Slamming his fist on the desk, he said, "I knew we shouldn't have green-lit this project when Dr. Wyatt proposed it."

Esmerelda tapped the top of the bottle. "In theory, this is a good idea. Unfortunately, the reality of it isn't."

Juan Carlos hated to ask the question, but because of the circumstances, he did anyway. "Could you use your gift to, maybe..." He stopped at the look she gave him. "I know. Your gifts come at a price."

"A high price," Esmerelda emphasized. Sighing, she said, "And I thought of that. There's something unnatural about it. I can't put my finger on it."

Juan Carlos leaned forward in interest. "What do you mean?"

Esmerelda took a deep breath before explaining. "When I put a pill on a big piece of pork fat, it dissolved instantly into it. Within minutes, the fat was pulsing and then exploded."

Juan Carlos picked up his tablet and pulled up the data from Dr. Wyatt's project. "What? The simulations didn't show people exploding."

Esmerelda's face twisted in disgust. "I don't care what type of miracle drug this was supposed to be. It shouldn't act that fast. It's not natural."

Eyeing Esmerelda, Juan Carlos continued scrolling through the information. "When you say unnatural, what exactly do you mean?"

Esmerelda hugged herself. "I looked at the data, and it should work, but not that fast. It's like the reaction was sped up."

Setting the tablet down, Juan Carlos pondered. "You know, we didn't think about that. In his reports, Dr. Wyatt said the results would take days, weeks even."

"Do you think someone was trying to sabotage the project?" Esmerelda thought for a moment. "I didn't find anything in the pill that wasn't supposed to be there, and I didn't sense any mystical elements."

Juan Carlos picked up his tablet and began tapping away. "Still, it's worth looking into. If there was a catalyst agent in it that we didn't catch or know to look for, that could be the key. I'll have Dr. Gingerman look into it."

"How's Diego doing?" Esmerelda asked, changing the subject.

Putting the tablet down again, Juan Carlos sighed. "As well as can be expected. He said he was still hurting, but I think he needs some time to process everything. I wish I could fix it all for him. He feels guilty for not stopping them."

"I know, but you can't fix everything for him. He has to stand on his own two feet." Esmerelda's words reminded Juan Carlos that the truth could hurt. "You raised him right. He'll ask for help when he needs it, and when he doesn't, be there for him."

"I know. It's that he always thinks of others before himself." Juan Carlos chuckled at a fond memory. "Remember his eighteenth birthday?"

"I've never seen you so mad or cry so hard." The edges of Esmerelda's lips curled into a slight smile. "He left at seven in the morning and didn't get home until almost six."

Juan Carlos shook his head. "I figured he was out celebrating with his friends. I was so focused on making his birthday dinner that I didn't notice he was gone. It was when you showed up with Freddy that I realized the time."

"You didn't even realize he wasn't home. I remember you yelling for him to get ready before you went to shower." Esmerelda covered her mouth to hide the tiny laugh she let out. "It was when you came out and asked where Diego was and Freddy told you he wasn't here that you freaked."

"At least he answered my call and kept me updated with texts," Juan Carlos defended.

"Until he didn't, and he wouldn't tell you what he was doing that was more important than his party." Esmerelda smirked. "People started showing up. You wouldn't let them eat or leave until Diego showed up."

"What would you have done?" Esmerelda's look told him she would have done the same. "He came bursting in, all sweaty and nasty."

Juan Carlos put his head in his head. "I was so mad."

Esmerelda cleared her throat and did her best impression of an angry Juan Carlos. "Look who we have here! El reino de la casa. Your majesty, I hope we haven't inconvenienced you by celebrating your birthday. Would you like to tell everyone why you've kept them waiting?"

With fondness, Juan Carlos said, "His hand was trembling when he handed me the folder. I looked at the papers inside, not understanding what they meant."

Esmerelda's voice went soft, choked with emotion. "I took them from you and read them. You were so impatient waiting for the answer. I still remember your face when I told you."

Juan Carlos took a deep breath to hold back the tears. "They had given him the run around at the courthouse all day. Sending him to this building, then to this office, and then that office."

"He had his last name changed to Sanz." A tear ran down Esmerelda's cheek.

"It was his birthday, but he gave me the best present in the world. How can you be mad at that?" Tears were streaming from Juan Carlos's eyes.

Esmerelda threw her head back in a hearty laugh. "Oh, you got mad, remember? Leave it to your boy to end up on the news on his birthday."

Juan Carlos wiped at his eyes. "Joder, look at us crying like we're in a telenovela. Remind me to yell at Diego for ruining my makeup."

"I could give him a tail if you want," Esmerelda joked.

Juan Carlos erupted into laughter. "You know I caught him trying to look at his butt to see if you had given him a tail this morning?"

CHAPTER 28

DIEGO USED THE EXCUSE OF STILL BEING IN pain to stay home the next day. The truth was that whatever Esmerelda had given him pretty much healed him. He really wanted to be home when his suit finished repairing and upgrading itself. The damage had been more extensive than they had originally thought. If only he could give it some of Esmerelda's herbs.

This was the fifth time before lunch that he had gone to check on it in its pod. Every time he saw the growing pile of damaged microbots, he felt guilty. Not only could he have died, but his baby could have been destroyed. He hated to admit it, but he understood Dr. Wyatt, just a little. If only his parents had cared about their creation half as much.

He hated to admit it, but Juan Carlos was right. They had done the best they could. They were kids who thought they were grown and had the world figured out. They didn't, but they had each other. That was good enough for the first thirteen or so of Diego's life. That's when things changed.

That's when he noticed it. The growing rift between his parents. The tiny tremors of resentment between them—the pills his mother constantly took to ease her headaches—the empty beer bottles he'd clean up after his father passed out drunk after work—the fights in Spanish that they didn't know he understood.

By fourteen, he had learned to fend for himself, doing his own laundry and scrounging for food. Some days, the free meal he got at school was the only meal he got. His mother became more distant and his father stayed out late drinking, if he came home at all. Diego started skipping school, too embarrassed to be seen in the rags he had as clothes that were too small for him.

It was around that time he was caught spray painting Juan Carlos's house. Diego could see that he was mad, but not at Diego, really. Diego hadn't run or put up much of a fight against Juan Carlos dragging him in to write "Fuck the police" a hundred times because someone had cared enough to actually pay attention to him.

When that sandwich appeared in front of him, Diego almost cried. That's why Diego showed up the next day to try and scrub off his handy work. He had found an old bucket and rags rummaging through the trash. With water stolen from Juan Carlos's hose, he scrubbed that wall for hours, not making any kind of progress in removing the paint.

Eventually, Juan Carlos came out, and saw what he was doing—and the lack of progress he was making. He looked at Diego, really looked at Diego, and then walked down the street. He came back a half hour later with the paint and supplies. He set them in front of Diego, then went inside.

Diego pulled out the rollers, brushes, and paint pan. He had never painted before, but he assumed it was easy. If he could have only gotten the paint can to open. For five minutes,

Diego tried to open the paint, clawing at the lid with his nails, cursing in both English and Spanish.

"What in the hell do you think you're doing?" Diego froze when he heard Juan Carlos's exasperated question. Diego was holding the can with both hands up above his head and was getting ready to smash it on the ground. "Ay, dios mio. You are not this stupid."

Juan Carlos snatched the can from Diego, sat it down on the ground, and, after pulling a small screwdriver from his pocket, popped the lid of the can off. "Grab me that stick out of the bag, please." Diego did as he was told. "You have to stir the paint first," Juan Carlos instructed, moving the wooden stick through the paint. "Then, we can start."

There was more to it than that, Diego would learn later on. This was good for what they had to do, and it shouldn't have taken two hours. Juan Carlos had dragged it out, talking to Diego. Every now and then, when Diego said something, Juan Carlos would stop and look at him, as if he actually was seeing Diego. After they finished, Juan Carlos had made them both something to eat.

That was when Juan Carlos coaxed the confession out of Diego that he wasn't going to school and about his parents. Diego cringed at the anger that was behind those kind and compassionate eyes. Diego nearly ran out of the tiny house when Juan Carlos slammed his hand on the table.

"You'll go to school every day and come back here to do your homework. In fact, I'm taking you there myself tomorrow," Juan Carlos proclaimed.

Juan Carlos had walked Diego home that night. Luckily, neither of his parents had been home. Diego could imagine the hell he would have let out on them. They weren't there the next morning, either, when Juan Carlos showed up at the apartment to take him to school.

Juan Carlos didn't have to do it, but he took Diego under his wing. After school, Diego showed up at Juan Carlos's house and did his homework before they had dinner together. Before it got too late, Diego would reluctantly go home, never knowing what he'd be walking into.

His mother had started doing harder stuff, and things in the apartment started turning up missing. His father rarely ever came home. When he did, it was because he had no other place to go. His parents ended up fighting like cats and dogs on those occasions. Diego would lock himself in his room and wish that Juan Carlos was his parent.

On such rare occasions, Diego's father had noticed the changes in Diego. Juan Carlos had him eating right and exercising. The pudgy kid his father knew was now a svelte young man. He was wearing decent clothing without holes in them and shoes that weren't worn down to the sole.

"Look at my boy, all pretty and shit. I bet you're breaking all the girls' hearts like your old man," his father had slurred. He tugged at Diego's shirt. "Where did you get the money for this shit? You selling drugs?"

Diego hadn't expected the punch to his jaw that knocked him to the ground when he said Juan Carlos's name. "Maricon!" His father spat on him. His mother just laid there on the broken couch, zoned out on her latest score. "I'm going to beat the gay out of you!"

Diego didn't remember what happened next. He didn't remember running from the apartment or down the stairs to the street. He somehow ended up at Juan Carlos's place, having his tears wiped away by a gentle hand. He vaguely remembered blubbering to Juan Carlos about what happened.

"I got you. You can stay here for as long as you need to," Juan Carlos told him, patting his leg.

Diego had never left. Juan Carlos had taken care of him ever since. *If it hadn't been for Juan Carlos.* Diego dipped his hand into the growing pile of discarded microbots. *If it hadn't been for him, who knows what would have happened to me?*

The pod beeped. The suit was a third of its size. Diego knew it would heal itself. It would take time, like it took time for Diego to heal. Diego raised his hand from the pile, damaged microbots spilling through his fingers. A tendril from the suit came out and ran over Diego's hand, scooping up the loose microbots.

"I'm sorry," Diego said to the suit. "I'll protect you better from now on. I promise." The tendril dove into the pile, using the broken microbots for material for the suit's repair. "I'll come back and check on you in a bit." Diego walked away. "I need to do something nice for Juan Carlos."

CHAPTER 29

A LEX WASN'T SURE HE SHOULD CLICK THE link that was texted to him. The number was blocked and the message only read:

[Unknown: If you really want to know what kind of people you work for.]

Curiosity got the better of him, though. He lightly pressed on the link to preview it. It took him to one of the local station's YouTube channels. Figuring it was safe, he opened the link.

Alex wasn't sure what he was watching at first. The video was over ten years old and titled *Young Latino Discriminated Against at the Courthouse*. The video had a couple of million views and over fifty thousand comments and shares. Wondering what that had to do with Juan Carlos and Diego, Alex started the video.

The page buffered a bit, then came to life. A young female reporter with the prerequisite blue blazer and black pencil skirt appeared on the screen. Her long brown hair looked as if it was teased to perfection, with curls and waves cascading down her head to her shoulders. It was the perfect frame of her softly done-up makeup.

She was in the hall of the local courthouse, holding up a big boxy microphone to her mouth. She began. "This is Miranda Richardson reporting from the Morgan City Courthouse. I'm here with Judge Doug Trainer, the man that wants to be your next mayor."

She turned sharply at the waist to face the man in a double-breasted, pinstripe suit. He reminded Alex of a living Ken doll with his perfectly gelled hair combed to the side, blue eyes, and broad shoulders. It took a moment for Alex to place the same man that was the mayor of Morgan City for the past twelve or so years.

"Judge Trainer, you're running on being a man of the people. To rid our city of corruption and discrimination." Miranda put the microphone in front of Judge Trainer for confirmation.

Alex was expecting there to be a twinkle when Judge Trainer flashed a smile. "That I am, Miranda. Our current mayor has failed this city. Crime is rampant in the streets. Minorities are discriminated against when they try to get grants, business licenses, or—"

"Their name changed," Miranda interrupted.

"Or their name changed," Judge Trainer repeated, puzzled by Miranda's example.

Miranda took the microphone back to herself. Still facing Judge Trainer, her eyes went to the camera. "I got married last month."

Not knowing where she was going with her story, Judge Trainer said, "Congratulations."

She looked at Judge Trainer briefly when she said, "Thank you." Her eyes went back to the camera. "I had my name changed. Do you know how long it took me to get my name changed?" She didn't give Judge Trainer a chance to answer. "After sending in all the appropriate paperwork, an hour."

The microphone was back in front of Judge Trainer, who answered confidently, "We try to be expedient with such minor, yet important, details."

"Yes, it was a very simple process. I got my hearing the same day. It was quite expeditious." Miranda turned fully to the camera. "Imagine my surprise when we were coming up the court steps and found a young Latino boy crying on the courthouse steps because after weeks of planning and making sure all his paperwork was right, the hearing he had sched-uled to have his name changed was canceled because, as he was told, his paperwork wasn't right."

Miranda motioned for someone to come toward her, and the camera panned out. A lanky young Latinx boy with red-rimmed eyes and slumped shoulders stepped forward to stand on the other side of Miranda. Alex squinted at the video. He recognized the young man, but he couldn't place from where.

"This is Diego Torres. He's been here since the courts opened at nine this morning, trying to get his last name changed. It is nearly five now." Miranda turned to the young man, her voice turning reporter soft. "Diego, could you tell our viewers why exactly you're changing your name?"

With his big brown eyes staring into the camera, he leaned forward to speak into the microphone. "Um, today is my birthday," he began, his voice shaky with nervousness. "I've been planning this for weeks so that today, when I turned eighteen, I could change my last name to that of the wonderful man that raised me."

Miranda took the microphone back long enough to ask, "Happy birthday, but why is this important to you?"

"Because he didn't have to take me in off the streets." Alex could see the tears welling up in the boy's eyes. "He's just the best mom and dad a kid could have. He made sure I had food in my belly, a place to sleep, clothes on my back. He taught me to work for the betterment of our community, made sure I went to school. He saved my life. He made sure I had a future."

Alex saw the boy's face turn to one of disappointment. "He doesn't know I'm doing this. He's at home right now, getting this big party ready for me. I wanted to do this as a way to say thank you to him. For all he's done for me. He means the world to me. I wanted to show him that just because we're not family by blood, I'll always think of him as my family."

Miranda pulled the microphone away and stared directly into the camera as she spoke. "A very touching and emotional story. Wouldn't you agree, Judge Trainer?"

She thrust the microphone at Judge Trainer. "Yes, extremely emotional. Happy birthday, by the way. I'm sorry you've gone through that. This is the type of hassle and discrimination I aim to put a stop to when I am in office."

Miranda yanked the microphone back and stared directly into the camera. "I had our legal experts take a look at Mr. Torres's paperwork before the interview, and it seems all of Mr. Torres's paperwork is in order. We also followed Mr. Torres's paper trail. Just from the sign-in logs, we show he was in your office three times today, Judge Trainer. First thing this morning, then at one and three this afternoon. What do you have to say to that, Judge Trainer?"

Miranda thrust the microphone at the obviously uncomfortable Judge Trainer. He took a moment to compose himself, but in true politician fashion, he recovered quickly. "I am deeply horrified that this young man has been turned away from my office three times. Once is too many. I will be having a conversation with my staff to ensure things like this do not happen in the future. I will make this right."

Miranda snapped the microphone back to herself. She was facing the camera when she asked, "So you'll help this young man get his name changed today?"

Alex wondered how she hadn't hit someone with how she was thrusting that microphone about. "I, uh, sure. Come with me to my office. We'll get it done right now."

The clip cut, and now Judge Trainer was standing with an awkward arm around the young man's shoulder. The young man wore a smile stretched from ear to ear. Miranda was in front of the two, but off to the side. "With the paperwork certified by Judge Trainer, this young man now has a new last name. Would you like to share with our audience at home your new name?"

Just as before, the young man leaned forward to talk into the microphone and stare up into the camera. "Diego Sanz."

Miranda snapped the microphone back to herself. "There you have it, ladies and gentlemen. With the quick action of Judge Trainer setting everything right for this young man on his birthday, he can go home and show the man he calls dad his new name. Is there anything you'd like to say to him on air?"

She thrust the microphone back at Diego. "Oh, I don't call him dad. I call him mamacita. His name is Juan Carlos Sanz."

If Miranda was uncomfortable when she took the microphone back, she didn't show it. "Well, Mamacita Sanz, I would just like to add that I've spent just a little while with your boy, and you did an excellent job. This is Miranda Richardson signing off."

The video ended. Alex wasn't sure why someone had sent him the video with that ominous message. If the video was supposed to show Diego and Juan Carlos in a bad light, it failed. It showed what big hearts they had—how much they loved each other. Diego had spent his entire birthday trying to get his name changed so he could be a Sanz just like Juan

Carlos because of how much Juan Carlos meant to him. What was bad about that?

Alex set his phone down on the desk. *I wonder who sent that.*

"Dion, did you do that special task I asked you to do?" Juan Carlos asked, stepping out of his office.

Dion stopped typing and gave him a side-eye. "Of course I did, and I'm not sure that was fair, given your bet with Esmerelda."

Juan Carlos held his hand out to examine his nails. "All is fair in love and war. Besides, you owed me since you told Esmerelda about Detective Heath."

"You told me not to tell Diego, not Esmerelda," Dion defended.

"Just remember who signs your paychecks," Juan Carlos warned.

"Diego does, and Esmerelda's getting me the number to that hot new barista at the coffee shop next door," Dion answered swiftly.

"Is that why you've developed that sudden latte addiction?" Juan Carlos smirked.

"Don't you dare." Dion glared at him when she saw the look in his eyes.

"I would never, but if Diego found out you had the hots for a young lady at the coffee shop..." Juan Carlos intentionally left the sentence unfinished.

Dion slit her eyes at him. "I hate you; you know that."

Juan Carlos fluttered his hands about. "Remember, if Diego is focused on his love life, he won't mettle in ours."

Dion massaged her temples. "I'm just lucky I'm not still in litigation."

"Are we Team Diego now?"

Dion glared at Juan Carlos. "Team Diego."

CHAPTER 30

ALEX STOOD WATCHING FREDDY DANCE around the ring in his boxing shorts and gloves. Sweat poured off Freddy's body as he moved in quickly to attack his opponent with quick jabs, uppercuts, and cross hits before he moved back to guard his own body. Then he was in again, performing a new combination of punches.

Alex hadn't expected this when Freddy called him back and asked him to meet him here. Alex mentally groaned when Freddy came out of the gym shirtless, letting everyone see his smooth cocoa brown skin stretched tight over the mountain and valleys of his heaving abdominal muscles.

"Sorry," Freddy said, pulling Alex into the gym with him. "I'm running late. I just have one more exhibition, then I can shower and change."

"Oh, God," Alex had muttered under his breath at the thought of water cascading over Freddy's body. The water in wild rivers as it gushed through the channels of Freddy's muscles. "I need to get laid."

Alex was sure he had spoken too softly for Freddy to hear, but he turned back to give Alex a salacious smile and a wink. Alex felt his cheeks warm, his groin stir. He wanted more than sex, but Freddy stirred something primal, almost animal, in Alex. It grew as he watched Freddy in the ring, his body glistening with sweat.

"That," Freddy hit the punching bag one last time, "is some of what you'll learn if you decide to take classes here." Freddy moved to the ropes to address the small group of people gathered to watch him. "We'll put you through intense workouts and help you with your nutrition."

While Freddy was addressing the group, Alex found himself drawn to the wolf tattoo on Freddy's left pec. He couldn't take his eyes off the detailed artwork while Freddy was answering questions from the tiny crowd. He hadn't noticed it before, but the head of a wolf was howling. He could almost hear it.

Alex thought his eyes were playing tricks on him. The wolf began to move, the head lowering from its howl. Its head turned, and Alex swore it was looking right at him, staring deep into his soul. The eyes glowed yellow and its mouth turned into a snarl. It looked like it was coming to him.

Alex took a fearful step back. The wolf was now standing, hackles raised, poised to attack. Alex felt the fear in the pit of his stomach. He swore he could hear the wolf growl at him, feel it stalking toward him. Alex was certain the wolf was going to attack him and tear out his throat at any moment.

"Alex?" Alex startled at Freddy calling his name from the ring. "Are you okay?"

Alex shook the image of the wolf out of his head. He looked at Freddy's tattoo. It was there, unchanged, howling up at the moon. "Yeah, I think I just drifted off for a minute."

Freddy climbed out of the ring. "Cool. I'm just going to grab a quick shower and we can go grab a bite to eat." Freddy winked at Alex. "Feel free to look at my ass as I walk away." Freddy headed to the locker room, giving an exaggerated wiggle of his butt. "I hope you're enjoying the view."

Alex shook his head, laughing. He couldn't decide if Freddy was too much or just enough. He obviously was very proud of his butt. It was a nice one if Alex had to judge it. It wasn't as nice as Shadow Guardian's. Or Diego's, for that matter. Now those were asses Alex could really appreciate.

"Hey." Alex was brought out of his fantasy by the sound of a gruff, husky voice. He turned to see a man in a sleeveless tee coming toward him. "Hey, you." Alex was about to turn and run, but the man was already there in front of him. "You're the guy that fixes shit, right?"

"Yes, I fix electronics," Alex was barely able to squeak out.

Alex nearly fainted when the man thrust out his hand to be shaken. "I want to thank you, man." Confused, Alex took the man's outstretched hand. "You fixed my kid's tablet. I couldn't afford to get him a new one, but you made his better than new."

Exhaling, Alex relaxed. "You're welcome. It was nothing. Anything I can do to help."

The man let go of Alex's hand and put his on his hips. "Really? Because you got my kid interested in electronics now, all that computer shit." The man worked his jaw in contemplation. "Do you think you could, I don't know, talk to him? Tell him what it takes to be a guy like you?"

"Hey, Alan!" The voice of another man cut Alex off. "Who are you talking to?" This man, shirtless and covered with a sheen of sweat, came jogging up. "What's up?' He nodded to Alex. "We working out or what?"

"Don't be rude, man." Alan punched the newcomer playfully on the arm. "Do you know who this is? This is the cat that fixed my son's tablet."

The newcomer looked Alex up and down. "Word? You fixed my phone. When my wife picked it up, she had my daughter with her. You got her interested in developing apps and stuff."

"Hey, guys!" Alan shouted over the sound of clacking weights and grunts. "Come meet this dude! He's the one that's been fixing all our electronics!"

Alex soon found himself surrounded by hot and sweaty men and women, each telling them how, after fixing something of theirs, Alex got their kids, little brothers, or sisters, interested in science. It was great and all, but overwhelming. Alex wasn't used to being the center of attention.

"Guys! Can I get to my date?" Freddy yelled over the crowd.

"Date?" someone shouted back at Freddy. "You don't date, you—"

"Say it, and you're in the ring with me tomorrow." Freddy nudged his way to Alex. "Look at you being Mister Popular." Freddy saw the pleading in Alex's eyes. "Okay, everyone, I got to get my boy here to our dinner reservation."

"What about talking to our kids?" someone called out from the crowd. "When's he going to do that?"

Freddy raised an eyebrow at Alex. "Um, how about this Saturday?" Alex looked at Freddy for confirmation. "How about we do it this Saturday, here at the gym?"

"That works." Freddy patted Alex on the back. "You can use one of the workout studios. I'll clear it with the boss tomorrow." Freddy looked into the crowd and addressed them. "Now, can I take my date out?"

"What was that all about? How do they know you?" Freddy asked, ignoring the catcalls and whistles behind them.

"I, uh, guess a small pebble can make a big splash." Alex shrugged. "I got their kids interested in science by fixing their stuff."

"Cool, well, here we are." Freddy stopped in front of a food truck. "This truck has the best burgers anywhere." Freddy absently scratched the tattoo on his chest through his shirt. "Go all out. My treat."

Freddy and Alex sat outside the truck, eating and talking. They talked until the food truck packed up and left. They casually strolled back to the building, Freddy scratching at his tattoo. When they reached the front of the building, they stood awkwardly in front of each other. Freddy started rocking on the heels of his feet uncomfortably.

"Alex, you're a great guy," he said. Alex knew this speech; this wasn't the first time someone had said it to him. "I don't think it's a good idea for us to be more than friends. You know, with us living in the same building and the whole Diego thing."

"Diego and me are not a thing. He and I have never been a thing," Alex said defensively.

Freddy gave Alex a questioning look. "I meant because you work for him, and technically, I do, too." Freddy scratched at his chest. "Anyways, I hope this doesn't affect you coming down to the gym and talking to the kids, and I hope we can still be friends."

Alex laughed it off. "Of course, we can still be friends, and of course, I'll still come speak to the kids."

"Great." Freddy hugged Alex. "I got to get going. I can't wait to move in here. I'll catch you later. Let's do this again soon."

"Yeah, I'd like that." Alex stepped back, not exactly disappointed or relieved. "Maybe you can teach me to box."

Freddy winked at him. "Maybe. Good night."

"Good night." Alex watched Freddy walking away, then got an idea. "Just so you know, I'm looking at your ass!" he yelled out at Freddy.

"It's a great ass, isn't it?" Freddy called back.

CHAPTER 31

PAPA WOKE UP IN HIS MAKESHIFT BEDROOM. Honey was curled up against him, snoring softly. They had had an adventurous night of robbing and destroying stores in their harnesses and bear masks while Teddy had been tasked with making the new batch of Build and Burn. It was the only thing he trusted Teddy to do.

Word had gotten out about them roaming the streets because people ran when they saw them. They had nothing to worry about, being that the police rarely came to this part of town, and when they did, it was only in the daytime. They struck fear in the hearts of everyone and, apparently, Shadow Guardian, because he was nowhere to be seen.

Teddy had scowled at them when they returned and started mumbling under his breath while he worked. Teddy made a show of stomping into the back while they celebrated. It was then that Papa finally decided that it was time to get rid of Teddy. That was why Honey was with him now.

Honey was the only other person that knew how to properly make Build and Burn. That was why he had brought Honey into his room, fucked him senseless, and allowed him to stay the night. He needed Honey on his side. He needed Honey loyal to him and not to the insolent bear that didn't share his vision.

"Good morning. Last night was awesome." Honey yawned, stroking Papa's chest.

"It was," Papa reluctantly agreed. "You know we could have fun like that more often if we didn't have Teddy ruining it. I don't think he's completely on board with our vision of a Build and Burn future," Papa ventured.

Honey snuggled close to Papa. "He is. He's just not fun like us."

"Is he?" Papa stroked Honey's back. "He complains about the food we get. He made that scene last night when we came back. He hates that I have my pet that fits our leather, and I'm fairly certain he plans on releasing our test subjects." Honey made slow circles with his finger on Papa's chest. "Of course, you know he disapproves of me and you."

Honey's finger stopped. "How do we get rid of him?"

Papa grinned, knowing he had just solidified Honey's allegiance. "That I don't know yet, but we need to neutralize him. Permanently."

Honey's voice turned cruel. "It won't be easy. Build and Burn has made us unusually strong. Even our skin toughens with each injection." Honey strummed his fingers on Papa's chest. "We'll have to poison his doses."

Papa felt a stirring in his loins. "Can you do it? What about Build and Burn? Can you make it?"

"Of course." Papa's cock sprang to life from Honey's devious words. "I know the formula by heart."

Papa groaned, putting his hand on Honey's head. "Oh, Honey, take care of this for me." Papa pushed Honey down to his engorged cock. "Then we'll take care of Teddy."

Teddy quietly stalked into the locker room. He had gone to sleep alone, and woken up alone, which meant Honey had spent the night with Papa. They had been friends once, but now Honey spent all his free time with Papa, following him around like some lap dog. What he and Honey had, could have had, was gone with the push of that needle.

That was okay. He had Sugar now. Sugar would satisfy his sweet tooth. His sweet Sugar that was sleeping on the floor with that bitter creature they brought back with them. That bitter thing would serve as Teddy's test subject to perfect Build and Burn, and once perfected, Teddy would have his Sugar Bear.

"Why are you staring at me while I sleep? It's creepy," Sugar said behind closed eyes.

"I wanted to check on you," Teddy fumbled with his words. "I, uh, didn't mean to disturb you. I'll go."

"Wait." Teddy watched as he stretched his nearly naked body. What he wouldn't give to taste the sweetness from that skin. "Keep me company." Sugar sat up. Pulling his knees to his chest, hiding most of his body from Teddy. "Why do you keep calling me Sugar? My name is Joshua."

Teddy looked away from Joshua, embarrassed. "I, uh, like sugar, and I like you."

"Don't you think it's a bit early for pet names? Especially since I have a boyfriend?" Anger and shame filled Teddy with Joshua's soft admonishment. "Tell you what: you, and only you, can call me Sugar if you take me to my boyfriend so I can break up with him so that I can be with you."

Teddy perked up. "I can break him. Tell me who he is. I'll break him up into tiny pieces for you."

Joshua panicked. "No! I need to do it in person. He deserves that. Closure, you know?" Joshua watched Teddy trying to make sense of the words. "It's the only way we can be together."

"You, you want to be with me? Really? Me?" Teddy stammered out. He could feel his cheeks redden with embarrassment.

Joshua flashed Teddy a lecherous grin. "Yeah, you're sweet and cute. Do you think you could take me today? So we can be together?" Joshua waggled his eyebrows to drive home the point.

"I'll see what I can do." Teddy took a step back, nervous. "I need to go." Teddy was about to flee when he added quietly, "I want to be with you, too." Then he was gone.

CHAPTER 32

D IEGO SAT IN HIS OFFICE. HE HAD GOTTEN up early and tested the new suit modifications and was impressed with what Alex had come up with. He was itching to try them out in the field, but he had to go into the office today. More importantly, he had no idea how to find Dr. Wyatt and his minions.

The day had been filled with expense reports, project presentations, meetings, and everything else that Diego loved to hate about running a company. By lunchtime, he had approved three promising new ventures, shut down a project that had yet to yield any return, and reviewed the projections for the next six months.

"Do you have a moment?" Diego looked up to see Juan Carlos in the doorway. He set his tablet aside and motioned Juan Carlos in. "I've got news about Dr. Wyatt." Juan Carlos settled in the chair across from Diego. "It seems he's branched out to petty larceny and robbery. He and one of his bears went out terrorizing the town last night—specifically the North Side."

"Where? Why are we just now finding out about it, and why wasn't it in the news?" Diego asked, leaning forward.

"Because of where it was," Juan Carlos answered bluntly. "Robberies aren't news in North Side. The only reason I know about it is because it came across Aaron's desk as a possible lead for his investigation."

Diego cracked a smile. "Aaron? Who is Aaron?"

"The detective assigned to the warehouse robbery," Juan Carlos sighed. "Can we please focus? The police are doing the routine stuff about the robberies, filing reports for the insurance companies, but other than that, nothing more. Every call they got last night wasn't responded to until this morning. What if someone got hurt, or worse, killed?"

"Get me a list of the businesses. Maybe we can figure out where Dr. Wyatt is hiding by seeing where he hit." Diego was doing his best to hide his concern for Alex.

"Yes, but there are a lot of abandoned buildings in that area. We'll need more information," Juan Carlos answered. Juan Carlos thought for a moment. "Esmerelda and Freddy."

"What about them?" Diego asked.

"I'll have them go ask around. The people aren't talking to the police, but they'll talk to Esmerelda," Juan Carlos answered.

"Because she's a," Diego paused at the glare Juan Carlos was giving him, "Gitana."

Juan Carlos stood. "Very good. I'll give her a call. Now the other thing I had to talk to you about, meet me in Alex's office after lunch. I have him working on a special project I think you'll like."

"Do you think he knows?" Diego asked.

"If he does, he hasn't let on." Juan Carlos thought for a moment. "I don't think he does, so you still have a shot as Diego."

"He works for me. You know what an HR mess that would be," Diego countered, not wanting to have this argument.

"Good thing I'm good at cleaning up your messes." Juan Carlos smiled wickedly. Tapping his fingers on Diego's desk, he said, "I've learned a few of your business tricks over the years. As of this morning, he works for me and my consulting company. In fact, several of the people that were stagnant in the company now work for it."

Diego sighed. "It's a loophole and not a big one. The risk isn't worth the price."

Juan Carlos looked at Diego pointedly. "It better be with the amount you pay us. Now quit wearing your ass as a hat and make your move before Alex is off the board. Esmeralda told me he went on a date with Freddy last night."

Juan Carlos turned and left, leaving Diego to ponder the news. How would it work? How would he explain the nights he couldn't see Alex? It wouldn't be fair to Alex. He couldn't do that to Alex. Then another important question hit Diego, one Juan Carlos had deflected deftly.

"Why are you and the detective on a first name business?" Diego called out just as Juan Carlos was about to exit the door. Diego laughed when Juan Carlos answered by raising one arm up, middle finger extended. "We're going to revisit this," Diego called out before his office door was shut.

CHAPTER 33

AS ALEX HEADED TO WORK THAT MORNING, the state of the block after turning the corner shocked him. Someone had destroyed storefronts, police had walled businesses off with police tape, and the people were asking, in hushed tones, where the shadow guy was. Why hadn't he stopped the wackos who did this?

Alex couldn't help but wonder if Shadow Guardian was staying away because of him. He knew he was being presumptuous, but why else wouldn't Shadow Guardian have shown up? He was lost, pondering that thought, when he reached for Benny's nightly bottle to find it wasn't there. Then Alex nearly jumped out of his skin when the improbable happened. Benny spoke.

"I threw that shit out last night when I started seeing things," he told Alex. "Saw some funny-looking bears coming out of that old gym last night." He pointed at the boarded-up building. "Figured it was time to get clean. When you start seeing man-bears, you know it's time to get clean."

Alex dismissed it as some drunken hallucination, as Benny had. Then he heard the people on the train talking about the two men in bear masks—how the police ignored their calls for help. The latter was the norm, so was crime. But men in bear masks rampaging through the streets? That was new.

What Benny had told him weighed heavily on Alex as he started his day at work. He worked on the new project Juan Carlos had waiting for him, but he couldn't get what he heard out of his head. He wasn't sure what to do. He could call the police, but they had proven they didn't care. The only thing he could do was find a way to tell Shadow Guardian.

Alex went over the specifications, not really understanding what Juan Carlos wanted. He leaned back and reread the email over and over again, then looked at the design specs. Going back and forth between the two, Alex finally realized what he was looking at wasn't what Juan Carlos wanted.

Once he realized that, the solution was simple. Figure out how to get Juan Carlos what he wanted, then work it into the design, just as he had with the suit. Working outside of the confines of the design, Alex finally made headway. He wasn't sure if he could use the suit technology for it, but Alex took a risk.

By lunchtime, he had the preliminaries done. It wasn't quite a working model yet, but it was something he could show Diego and Juan Carlos when they came in later. In the meantime, he could work on his personal problem—trying to figure out a way to contact Shadow Guardian and tell him about the man-bears.

Nibbling on his food and pacing his office, Alex finally decided to get out of the office. He needed to clear his head. He needed to get a different perspective on the problem, so he took what was left of his lunch and headed upstairs to the rooftop garden, hoping to find inspiration among Juan Carlos's flowers.

By the time his lunch was over, Alex still had no clue how to contact Shadow Guardian. It wasn't like Alex could shoot him an email or press a special button on his watch. A spotlight with a message might work, but what would say? "Come see me?" That sounded more like a desperate psychotic message from an ex.

Alex was still mired in the problem while he was showing Diego and Juan Carlos what he had come up with for the project. He pointed out the changes he'd come up with. He answered their questions, but Juan Carlos must have sensed his turmoil because he stopped Alex mid-explanation.

"Alex, what's wrong?" Alex looked at Juan Carlos, then at the screens, trying to find the problem. "Not with the project." He put a hand on Alex's shoulder. "With you. Tell me."

"It's nothing," Alex lied, but repented under Juan Carlos's parental gaze. "I need to get a message to someone, but I don't know how." Juan Carlos gestured for Alex to continue. "Last night, two men with these bear masks robbed and destroyed a bunch of businesses on a block near my apartment."

"Did you see them?" Diego crossed the room in a blur, nearly knocking Juan Carlos over as he took Alex by the shoulders. "What do you know?"

Alex darted his eyes to Juan Carlos, then back to Diego's. "No. I didn't see them. I heard people talking and how the police ignored the calls."

"Did you hear anything? Like where they went?" Diego asked, almost frantic.

"Benny said he saw them come out of an abandoned gym. He thought it was a drunken hallucination," Alex answered, a bit frightened.

"What gym?" Diego's grip on Alex tightened. "What gym?"

"The abandoned one on fourth," Alex answered, confused. "Why is it so important to you?"

"Juan Carlos?" Diego looked at him.

Juan Carlos already had his phone to his ear. "On it. I'm calling Esmeralda now."

"What's going on?" Alex darted his head back and forth between the two men. "Don't you want to know who I was going to tell?"

Diego was grinning ear to ear. "You don't know how much you've helped us—how much time you've saved us! I could kiss you."

Alex's eyes went wide, and his body stiffened when Diego's lips pressed to his. It took just a moment for him to close his eyes and relax into the unexpected kiss. He felt the softness of Diego's lips on his, the gentle scratch of his stubble. It reminded Alex of the kiss he shared not too long ago. Then it hit him.

Diego pulled away. "Oh, my God. I'm so sorry. I don't know what came over me."

"Esmerelda, we have a lead," Juan Carlos said into the phone. "Oh, and you owe me fifty bucks."

CHAPTER 34

PAPA BEAR GLANCED BACK AT THE DOOR TO the locker room with a sneer. Teddy had been back there most of the day. He only came out for food, then rushed back under the guise of tending to the lab rats in the back. Papa knew the real reason he was back there. Teddy was planning to oust him, and those lab rats were somehow part of his plan.

Moving to the corner where Honey had made his little workshop, Papa passed Tyler. He crinkled his nose at the offending stench that came from the broken man. Teddy was right; he did need a bath. Papa made a mental note to have Honey hose the man off once they solved their Teddy Bear problem.

He found Honey with parts scattered around him, talking quietly to himself. Papa mentally cursed his luck. One of his bears was plotting against him; the other was rapidly losing his mind. Why hadn't he actually done the work to create Build and Burn? He knew what went in it, but not the delicate proportions.

Papa looked over Honey's shoulder. "What are you doing? You're supposed to be poisoning Teddy's Build and Burn."

Honey smiled proudly up at Papa. "Oh, hey! I'm on it, but I wanted to make us these in case something went wrong." Honey jumped to his feet. He picked up the strange metal contraption he was working on and held it out to Papa. "Here, try it on."

"What is it?" Papa eyed the thing. It looked like three sharp blades attached to a metal frame.

"I call it the bear claw," Honey answered excitedly. "Let me see your arm; I'll put it on you." Papa reluctantly stretched out his right hand. "It works two ways." Honey slipped the metal frame over Papa's hand and down his forearm to his elbow. "Perfect fit." Honey flipped levers and tightened the frame. "Now, the fingers." Honey slipped each finger into a strap. "Perfect."

Papa yanked his arm away. "What the hell am I going to do with this? We need to stop fucking around and get serious."

"I came up with this for DJC. They said it wasn't practical for what I designed it for," Honey explained further. His brows furrowed in concentration. "Why did I design it? I know it was for something they wanted, but I can't remember what."

"Honey, focus," Papa growled.

Honey shook his head as if clearing it out. "Right. Right. Remember, I stole those sword things from that one store last night?" Papa fought the urge to throttle Honey. "I severed the blades and attached them. Like it is now, you can use the blades on your arms like razors."

Honey moved behind Papa and lifted his arm up. "Now, move your thumb across your palm." Papa did, triggering the blades to snap forward. "Now you have razor-sharp bear claws," Honey laughed maniacally. "I haven't figured out how to make them retract automatically yet."

Papa waved his arm around. "I like this. Bloody."

"Yes." Honey jumped up and down excitedly. "Wait until you see what I got for me!" Honey rushed around Papa and pulled out a small tank. "I filled this tank with some extra sticky goo, like honey. I put it on my back and it pumps into this gun!" Honey slipped on the tank and waved the spray nozzle around. "I call it my honey trap!"

Papa did his best to quell his annoyance. "We're going to talk about this bear thing you're on. Now I need you to write down the formula for Build and Burn." Papa ran his finger over one of the blades, imagining it stained with Honey's blood.

"Oh, yeah, sure." Honey started looking around for something to write with and on. "I'll get right on that. I just need to find something to write on."

"In the office," Papa said through gritted teeth. Carefully gripping one of the blades with two fingers, he pulled the blade back until it locked back into place. "Go do it now before you forget."

Honey slipped off his tank. "Yeah, right away. Right now. What are you going to do?"

"I'm going to see what our Teddy is up to." Papa pushed the last blade back in place. "Maybe I'll show him what my new little toy can do."

Teddy sat cross-legged in front of Joshua. "I think we can go tonight. They'll go out and terrorize the city. Then I can sneak you out."

Joshua pretended to be excited. "That's great. Then I can break up with my boyfriend and we can be together. "

"You have to take the Build and Burn first. It's not safe to be with me if you're not on Build and Burn. Not this version, though. I have to fix it," Teddy warned, rocking back and forth.

"Can you just stop taking it?" Joshua glared at Phil when he rolled over, groaning at their conversation. "I mean, if you stop taking it, I don't have to take it."

Teddy shook his head emphatically. "No. I'm addicted. One dose, and that's it. You're hooked." Teddy gave Joshua a weak smile. "It's not all bad. I was big. Really big. Then Honey gave me the Build and Burn, and I woke up like this."

"Is it healthy to lose that much weight so fast?" There was genuine concern in Joshua's voice. "Can you cleanse your system?"

Teddy shrugged. "I guess it's healthy. Papa said it was. He says once you start, you can't stop." Teddy's eyes darted side-to-side. "Papa lies, though. Maybe I can sweat it out." Teddy looked over his shoulder toward the steam room. "Maybe I can sweat it out and get a sexy body like Honey or Papa."

"You have a sexy body now," Joshua responded. "You don't need to lose any more weight unless you want to."

Teddy shook his head emphatically. "No. I'm fat. I need to lose more weight for you." Teddy stood. "I need to be sexy for you." Teddy went to the steam room. "I will be sexy for you."

Teddy cranked up the temperature and then stepped in. Sitting down on the bench, Teddy closed his eyes and listened to the hiss of steam. The heat surrounded him. Sweat almost immediately started trickling down his skin. The urge to leave and inject himself again grew and grew, but he resisted.

I need to do this. For Sugar, Teddy told himself over and over.

Teddy was drenched and light-headed when he heard the door open again. He wiped the sweat from his brow and opened his eyes just in time to see Papa's fist come flying at him. He fell to the scalding hot floor. Teddy tried to lift himself up, but his arms were yanked behind him, and cold metal wrapped around his wrists, then his ankles.

"Not as satisfying as gutting you," he was vaguely aware of Papa saying above him. "But it'll do." The last thing Teddy saw before blacking out was Papa's steel-toed boot coming at his head.

CHAPTER 35

D AY SETTLED INTO NIGHT AS THE LAST VES-
tiges of dusk faded along the horizon. Shadow Guardian
crouched, perched on the neighboring building of the suppos-
edly abandoned gym. With the flicker of street lights coming
on, he stood and moved back to get a running start. He checked
his systems one last time.

"It's time," he said before sprinting off the building and
deploying his glider wings. "I'm on the roof," he announced
when he landed gently on the roof of the gym. "Where to now?"

"The rooftop access," Juan Carlos buzzed in his ear. "It
leads down into the gym locker room. That's where Esmeralda
believes the three hostages are."

"How does she know?" Shadow Guardian asked, quietly crossing the neglected asphalt top. "I'm here." Shadow
Guardian tested the knob. It struggled to turn under his grip.
"How does she know?" Shadow Guardian repeated, putting
force behind his words.

"She just does." Juan Carlos's tone told Shadow Guardian not to ask further. "I also have backup, just in case." Shadow Guardian wanted to ask who but didn't. He knew Juan Carlos would have some sort of backup plan he wouldn't tell him about. "When you're ready." Juan Carlos paused. "Ten cuidado."

"I will." Shadow Guardian pulled until the door broke free of its frame and swung open. "Here goes nothing." Shadow Guardian crept down the stairs, the suit automatically adjusting his vision for the darkness. Reaching the bottom of the stairs, he put his ear to the door. "I don't hear anything." Shadow Guardian tried the handle. "It's locked." He jiggled the handle again. "I'm going to have to break it down."

"Wait," Juan Carlos nearly screamed in his ear. "I have an idea: put your hand on the handle and let me try something." Shadow Guardian did as he asked. He felt the tingling of movement across his skin. He watched the handle be enveloped by his microbots. They retreated back into his skin. "Try it now," Juan Carlos said into his ear.

The door opened without resistance. "It worked. Nice; where did you learn that trick?"

"Focus," Juan Carlos ordered. "You have hostages and three bears to worry about."

Cautiously, Shadow Guardian stepped into the locker room. It was a typical locker room with rows of lockers and a bench down the middle. He stealthily moved down the first row. He willed away his fear as the adrenaline flooded his system. He took a deep filtered breath, then peered around the corner.

"I see the two guards," Shadow Guardian reported. "One of them is trying to break free of his chains; the other is just lying there." He scanned around for anyone else. "I think they're alone."

Shadow Guardian slowly moved toward the two. With each step, he paused to make sure he wasn't detected. The large, older man on the ground moved. Shadow Guardian froze. The younger man kept tugging at his chains as if he had the strength to break them. He felt guilty for not having rescued them sooner.

"Hey, behind you. I'm here to rescue you," Shadow Guardian called to them in a hushed whisper.

The large man sat up and looked at Shadow Guardian. He rolled his eyes. "Fuck, another freak. If I get out of this alive, I'm retiring."

"Shut up, Phil," the younger man hissed. "You've got to get Teddy out of the steam room. He's been in there for hours."

"Teddy? Is he the leather shop owner?" Shadow Guardian gripped the chain, letting Juan Carlos use the microbots to disassemble the chain. "Do you know where your kidnappers are?"

"Teddy is one of the kidnappers. The boy here has a crush on that one." Phil held out his wrists for Shadow Guardian. "He and the big hairy man were at each other's throats." Phil's chains snapped free. "He's probably roasted by now."

"Help me get him out of there. We can't let him die," Joshua pleaded as Shadow Guardian freed their legs.

Phil stood. He leaned back, cracking his back. "Fuck that, Joshua. Get me out of this freak show."

Joshua stood. "He's the only one that took care of us in here. He's just as much a victim as us."

"Help me, don't help me," Shadow Guardian growled quietly. "There are stairs in the back to the roof where you can hide until the police get here, but I'm not leaving Teddy in that steam room." Shadow Guardian moved back toward the steam room, Joshua on his heels.

"You two are nuts. I'm out of here." Phil continued past them.

Shadow Guardian pulled open the door, releasing a burst of hot air. Shadow Guardian and Joshua rushed in, finding Teddy chained up on the floor. "Grab him by the arms." Shadow

Guardian took his right side while Joshua took the left. "On the count of three, we'll drag him out." Joshua nodded. "One. Two. Three."

They lifted Teddy's limp body and pulled him out of the steam room. Once out, they gently lowered him to the floor. Shadow Guardian made quick work of the chains, then rolled him over onto his back. "Get him some water," Shadow Guardian instructed. "Then head upstairs with your buddy. We'll get him medical help as soon as I take care of the other two."

"He needs that stuff." Joshua thought for a moment. "That burn stuff they are taking."

"Build and Burn? That stuff is poison." Shadow Guardian stood. "Give him that, and you're just condemning him to death. At least with medical attention, he'll have a chance to live." Joshua nodded. "Now go, get him some water, then get upstairs."

Shadow Guardian left them, heading to the door to the gym. He peeked around the corner. He spotted a man who had to be the leather shop owner chained to a wall, but he saw no sign of Dr. Wyatt. He crept in, ducking into a side room when he saw the blond man that called himself Honey wander through the gym equipment.

"How long do you think we need to keep him in that steam room before he's roasted?" Shadow Guardian heard him say. "Just so you know, I'm not cleaning it up. You can make one of those test subjects in the back do it."

"Will you shut up?" another man shouted. "Now go get our doses so we can try out our new toys."

"Hell yeah!" Honey shouted. "I can't wait to see how they work."

"It's now or never," Shadow Guardian announced to Juan Carlos. "Do what you have to if it comes to it."

"I will. Let's pray I don't have to. I'm cutting the power now. Kick their asses," Juan Carlos responded.

The lights cut off, but the emergency lights immediately went into action, casting the gym in a red glow. "What the hell?" Shadow Guardian heard the man that used to be Dr. Wyatt exclaim. "I thought you hacked into the power grid."

Shadow Guardian moved out of the room and into the main gym. He brought his thumb and index finger together on his right hand, activating the tranquilizer dart gun. On his left, he brought his pinky and thumb to activate the electrical charge. His left display showed his charge levels, while his right had a targeting system for him.

"Papa! We have company!" Honey had spotted him and was bouncing up and down. He had a tank strapped to his back with a hose that connected to a spray nozzle clipped to his side. "Should we show him how much we love uninvited guests?"

The man he called Papa came into view. Shadow Guardian had a brief recollection of seeing the man before, when he was charging him right before Juan Carlos took over the suit. He had something shiny and sharp strapped to his arm. He laughed. "What are you supposed to be? Some sort of super-hero? Let's take care of this fool, so we can go out and have some fun."

Honey, in true old gunfighter-style stance, grabbed the spray nozzle from his hip and aimed at Shadow Guardian. Shadow Guardian raised his right arm and aimed, prepared to dodge whatever Honey was going to shoot. They each took a step closer, then another and another.

They were ten feet apart when Honey said, "I hope you stick around." Yellow goo came at Shadow Guardian. He jumped to the side, releasing one of his darts at Honey. Honey missed, coating the floor. Shadow Guardian heard the ping of metal when his dart hit one of the machines.

"No fair! Stay still!" Honey pouted before giving chase.

Shadow Guardian was back on his feet, maneuvering between the weight machines, benches, and weights. He picked up a twenty-five-pound weight and hurled it at Honey just as he was about to release another shot. Honey screeched, and his hand with the nozzle went up just as he pressed the trigger.

Honey scrambled away, narrowly missing being coated in his own sticky mess. Shadow Guardian picked up a forty-five-pound weight and hurled it at the retreating Honey, only to have the man called Papa yank him out of the way before the weight hit its target. Shadow Guardian maneuvered through the gym equipment, trying to get a clear shot.

"It's not nice to throw things," Papa snarled. "Enough playing around, Honey! Get him!"

Honey nodded, and the two made their way through the gym debris toward Shadow Guardian. Honey went left while Papa went right. They were trying to box him in, but Shadow Guardian had other plans. He stepped up onto one of the benches. The two men came charging at him.

At the very last second, before the two came crashing into him, Shadow Guardian leaped, doing a somersault in the air and landing some feet away from the crashing duo. He heard Papa let out a sound of annoyance, and Honey let out a howl of pain. He turned to see Papa charging him like a raging bull.

Shadow Guardian checked the charge levels. With his left hand extended, Shadow Guardian waited, then twirled out of the way and touched Papa's back as he passed. The man screamed in agony, but he didn't go down. Instead, he grabbed the offending arm by the wrist and slung Shadow Guardian across the room into the wall lined with mirrors.

Shadow Guardian fell to the floor, shards of glass raining around him. The suit absorbed most of the impact, but he still had the wind knocked out of him. He got to his feet to see

Papa barreling at him. Without thinking, Shadow Guardian leaped up and over him, doing a flip in the air, letting Papa crash into the wall.

Landing in a crouch, he took aim at the dazed man-beast with the dart gun, but before he could release, he heard Honey bellow, "Don't you hurt my Papa Bear!"

Shadow Guardian turned his head to see Honey running, ready to spray his fluid. He rolled out of the way, letting the yellow fluid land on the floor. In the meantime, Papa had regained his senses and let loose a horrific sound of frustration. Shadow Guardian turned his attention back to Papa.

Papa turned around. His nostrils flared, his teeth bared, cheeks red with anger, and eyes set on murder. Papa extended his arm to the side, then made a fist. Blades snapped into place. Papa was breathing heavily. From behind him, Shadow Guardian heard Honey cackling maniacally.

Shadow Guardian crouched on the ground. *I need to take one of them out. I can't keep fighting them both.*

Shadow Guardian stood and turned off his electrical charge. He tapped his hip to activate his shadow stars. He took off running toward Honey. He heard the thumping boots of Papa behind him. Honey raised his spray nozzle. Shadow Guardian leaped up and over Honey as the spray shot forth.

Shadow Guardian tucked into a ball in the air, then spun around and unfurled his body. He threw the shadow stars at Honey's back, rupturing the tank. Stumbling as he landed, Shadow Guardian saw thick liquid ooze explode all over Honey. The shot Honey had intended for Shadow Guardian had hit Papa.

"Honey!" Papa bellowed, his body coated in the yellow sticky mess. "Get me out of this! Honey!"

Honey couldn't hear him over his own screeching. Shadow Guardian couldn't believe his luck. He raised his right arm, aimed for an exposed patch of skin on Papa, and released the dart. It flew through the air, stopping only when it sank into Papa's tough skin. When it looked like it had no effect on Papa, Shadow Guardian released a second, then a third. On the fourth, Papa finally began slurring his rants.

Honey struggled in his gooey cocoon. "What did you do to him? I'm going to kill you! There will be nowhere you can hide from me!"

Shadow Guardian released four shots into Honey and waited until he passed out, head slumped over. "My God, is that what it takes to shut him up?" Shadow Guardian moved around and made sure both were knocked out. Tapping his temple, he opened the live feed for Juan Carlos. "They are out, but I'm not sure for how long."

"Get out of there," Juan Carlos ordered. "I called Aaron and gave him the heads up. They'll be there in ten minutes."

Shadow Guardian took off for the back. "What about the leather shop owner?"

"They'll free him. If they catch you there, they may open fire on you, thinking you're one of them." Juan Carlos's voice was urgent.

"Fine." Shadow Guardian raced through the locker room then up the stairs. "I'm heading to the roof now." Busting through the roof door, he startled the two security guards. "It's safe to go down. The police will be here soon." Shadow Guardian raised his left arm and shot a tendril to the building across the street.

"Wait!" Joshua called out. "Who are you?"

Shadow Guardian paused, debating on answering. "Shadow Guardian," he said before jumping off the building and swinging away.

CHAPTER 36

ALEX KNEW IT WASN'T A GOOD IDEA TO BE hanging out in the alley across from the abandoned gym in hopes of seeing Shadow Guardian. He had to, though, to be sure of his suspicions. If Shadow Guardian showed, then he knew that Diego was Shadow Guardian. If he didn't, then he'd have to find a way to get in touch with Shadow Guardian. Then he'd have to deal with the kiss between him and Diego.

Luckily, the streets were deserted. Most businesses were boarded up, having been destroyed the previous night. The rest had closed when the sun set for fear they would be next. People had rushed to get off the streets, fearful of encountering the man-bears on their rampage. Even the criminals were hiding in fear.

The sun dipped below the horizon. Shadows filled the streets as the lights cut on. Alex looked up into the sky, scanning to see the familiar figure. *Where is he?* Alex sucked his teeth. *Come on; it has to be you.*

Alex almost missed it—Shadow Guardian gliding from the top of the building he was on and landing on the gym's roof. *I knew it.* Alex bolted across the deserted street to the alley beside the gym. *What am I doing?*

Alex was making his way down the dark alley. He halted when he heard the growl of a dog. Two yellow eyes appeared low, near the ground, in the darkness. The growl grew louder. The eyes rose up. Alex took a cautious step back. Swallowing hard, Alex held down his panic as the eyes grew closer.

Alex counted to ten, then turned to run, only to crash into Esmerelda. "A dormir." She ran her fingers tips down Alex's face. His eyes closed, and his body went limp.

CHAPTER 37

SHADOW GUARDIAN GLIDED ONTO THE rooftop garden feeling proud of what he had done. Juan Carlos was waiting for him, arms crossed. Walking over to Juan Carlos, Shadow Guardian's mask receded. He could tell Juan Carlos was trying not to smile, but the smirk he was trying to hide eventually turned into a broad smile.

Juan Carlos threw his arms around Diego. "You lucked out tonight. I'm so glad you're safe."

Diego hugged Juan Carlos back. "Thanks to you and your enhancements. Did the police get them out of that gunk Honey was shooting?"

Juan Carlos patted his back before pulling away. "No. They sent over a sample for us to analyze. In the meantime, they are keeping the two sedated."

"What about Teddy?" Juan Carlos looked away. "What about Teddy?"

"They only found the two," Juan Carlos answered softly. "Teddy was gone by the time they got there. He apparently woke up and escaped."

"The hostages?" Diego prodded. "What about the hostages? Are they all okay?"

"The leather store owner is a bit off from the long-term exposure to Honey's pheromones, but that should wear off," Juan Carlos answered. "The two security guards were taken to the hospital to be checked out, but they seemed fine."

"What about Detective Heath?" Diego teased. "Did he ask you how you knew where they were? Or how they were subdued?"

"I told him exactly what Alex told us. Nothing more. I just told them after you were done with your little adventure." Juan Carlos crossed his arms. "Speaking of Alex, Esmerelda found him knocked out behind the gym. You might want to go check up on him."

"Is he okay?" Juan Carlos smirked at him. "I'll be back." Diego stopped mid-stride and turned back to Juan Carlos. "Esmerelda was my backup?"

CHAPTER 38

ALEX GROANED AS THE SLEEP LEFT HIM. HE squinted into the darkness, trying to remember what had happened. He reached up and rubbed his head, his fingers combing through his hair. The last thing he remembered was crossing the street and heading into the alley beside the gym. He had the vague recollection of encountering a dog, and then everything was just blank.

Alex tossed the sheets off. Swinging his legs over the bed, he sat up. "What happened? How did I get home?"

"That's what I'd like to know." Startled, Alex jumped back from the voice in the darkness. The owner of the voice stepped into the moonlight that streamed through his open bedroom window. "What were you doing there?"

Alex held a hand over his pulsing heart. "I, uh, was looking for you." It wasn't the whole truth, but it wasn't a complete lie, either. "What did I tell you about knocking?"

"What did I tell you about locking your window?" Shadow Guardian crossed his arms across his massive chest. "Now, why were you at the abandoned gym, and what happened?"

"Why were you there?" Alex mimicked Shadow Guardian, crossing his arms defiantly. "And what happened?" Alex glared smugly at him. "Oh, and that window was closed and locked, so how did you get in?"

"It was open when I got here. Whoever brought you home must have opened it." Shadow Guardian took a step forward. Alex smirked. Shadow Guardian sounded like a jealous lover. "Now, why were you there, and what happened?"

"I told you." Alex stood, hoping he was being perceived as obstinate when he was really sizing up Shadow Guardian. His height and build. "I was looking for you. The rest, I don't know."

Shadow Guardian uncrossed his arms. His stance relaxed with concern. "Were you hurt?" Shadow Guardian put a hand on Alex's shoulder, the other cupped Alex's face. "Tell me what happened?"

Alex leaned his face into Shadow Guardian's hand. "I wasn't hurt. The last thing I remember was hearing some dog growling. I turned to run and," Alex's face furled in concentration, "then I was here."

"Please, don't make me worry about you." Pulling his hands away, Shadow Guardian stepped back. "I told you we can't see each other anymore. It's not safe. Especially now."

"Why?" Alex asked, his voice pleading. "Maybe I could train and be your sidekick or something. Superheroes have those."

"I'm no superhero." The sternness in Shadow Guardian's voice made Alex cringe. "And you're not a sidekick. You're a hero." Shadow Guardian looked to the open window, then back to Alex. "Please, don't try to contact me again." He cupped Alex's face again. "Shadow Guardian cannot have a boyfriend. Goodbye."

Shadow Guardian let go of Alex's face and jumped out the window. Alex rushed to the window and watched the retreating figure flying into the night. "Shadow Guardian can't," Alex said, shutting the window. "Diego Sanz can."

CHAPTER 39

"DID YOU TALK TO YOUR DETECTIVE YET? Did they find Teddy?" Diego asked Juan Carlos as they strolled down to Alex's office for another update.

"Yes and no," Juan Carlos answered. "He did say the solvent we sent him did dissolve the chemical mess Honey created. Once they have it all off them, they'll be transporting them to a high-security hospital."

Diego shook his head. "They haven't had Build and Burn for nearly twenty hours. Maybe we can microdose them until we can find a cure?"

"I suggested as much, and the authorities agreed. We'll be sending dosages daily under armed guard." They stopped in front of Alex's office door. "You and Alex? Are you going to be okay?"

Diego stood a little straighter, trying not to show the pain he felt. "Yes. I told him last night that I couldn't have a boyfriend."

"Shadow Guardian told him that. You did not," Juan Carlos corrected.

"Come on. He said he wanted to show us something." Juan Carlos opened the door to find Alex in his usual spot typing away. "Alex, you said you had something to show us?"

"Come in. Come in." Alex motioned them in excitedly. Standing up and coming around his desk, he said, "I didn't say I had something to show you both. I said I had something to show you, Juan Carlos."

"Juan Carlos said you asked for me to come as well." Diego and Juan Carlos shared a puzzled look. "Why am I here?"

"So I can show Juan Carlos that I'm taking his advice," Alex answered as if it were obvious. "He told me to be a big boulder and make a big splash."

"I did," Juan Carlos said, perplexed. "What does that have to do with Diego?"

"This." Alex reached up and cupped the back of Diego's head and pulled him into a kiss. This time it was Diego's turn to be shocked, but he soon melted into the kiss. Putting his arms around Alex, he pulled him close.

Juan Carlos coughed uncomfortably. "I see that my presence here is no longer needed." He cracked open the door. "Remember, these walls are soundproof," he said before leaving and shutting the door behind him.

CHAPTER 40

E SMERELDA SAT DOWN IN THE CHAIR BESIDE
Freddy's bed. Not wanting to disturb him, she waited for
Freddy to sense her presence and wake up. It didn't take long
for Freddy to yawn and stretch. He immediately looked over
at Esmerelda with sleepy eyes and his trademark goofy smirk.

"How are you feeling?" Esmerelda couldn't mask the concern in her voice.

Freddy worked the taste of the sleep out of his mouth.
"Good. Good. Did we get them?"

Esmerelda raised an eyebrow. "You don't know? Freddy,
you almost attacked Alex last night. I had to put him and you
down to keep you from hurting him. What was the last thing
you remember?"

Freddy thought for a moment. "Changing and waiting
in the alley with you. Then I caught the scent of Alex and
nothing else."

"Why would your wolf try to go after Alex?" Esmerelda
questioned.

Freddy shrugged. "It acted funny when we went on that date. It felt like it was trying to claw its way out of my skin and attack him."

"When was the last time you fooled around with someone?" Esmerelda narrowed her eyes at her cousin. Trouble etched across Esmerelda's face when Freddy shrugged. "The wolf in you is getting stronger. We need to break the curse soon. You'll be thirty in two months, and you know what that means."

"I'll be a middle-aged struggling boxer slash artist?" Freddy joked.

Esmerelda slapped Freddy on the forehead. "Quit playing around. This is serious."

Freddy rubbed his head. "Ouch. I think you've been hanging around Juan Carlos too much."

Esmerelda stood. "Get some rest. I need to go pay someone a visit."

"Where are you going?" Freddy was casually petting his wolf tattoo.

Esmeralda looked at the wolf, then at Freddy. "I have a debt to call in."

EPILOGUE

TEDDY SAT HUDDLED IN THE DARKNESS OF the cave. His skin itched with the need of Build and Burn. He came to on the locker room floor, his Sugar gone. He had stumbled into the main gym to see Honey and Papa fighting the shadowy man from the other night. He fought the urge to join the fight and help his fellow bears.

They had betrayed him, though, and the shadowy man had hurt him that night. None of them deserved his help. He was certain they were the reason his Sugar was gone. That was why he snuck into the room that had the Build and Burn, grabbed as much as he could, and snuck out the side entrance to where his truck was.

He was going to go back for a second score, but a wolf howl had scared him. He jumped in the truck and drove off, heading out of the city and into the woods. He drove until he didn't see any semblance of human life, then kept driving until his truck no longer had the will to go on. Then he packed up everything he could and headed into the woods where he found this cave.

Here he would recover with his limited supply of Build and Burn. Here he would plot his revenge—on Papa for taking away his Honey, on Honey for abandoning him, on the shadowy man because he took his Sugar, and last but not least, Diego Sanz for allowing Build and Burn to be developed. He'd have his revenge on all of them!

Joshua roamed around his apartment aimlessly. He and Phil had been questioned for hours after being rescued. Doctors had poked and prodded them until he felt like a pincushion. It wasn't until Juan Carlos, the COO of DJC, showed up that they were finally discharged and allowed to go home.

He had heard of the Fear of God, but that was nothing compared to what he saw Juan Carlos do. He had heard people at DJC joke about the Fear of Juan Carlos; having seen it firsthand, he knew it was no joke. It was real, and it was scary.

Juan Carlos decided he and Phil had endured enough. He was taking them home where they could rest with their loved ones. When one of the officers guarding them, a huge gorilla of a man in full tactical gear, tried to stop them, Juan Carlos had the man cowering and nearly in tears.

He arranged for them to be taken home, apologizing for Diego's absence due to some rock climb injury. He promised to check in on them and told them to take as much time as they needed to recover from the whole horrible ordeal. They, of course, would be paid and compensated for their trauma.

Phil had asked about the money; he had asked about Teddy. Joshua wanted to defend the man that called him his Sugar Bear. He wanted to tell them how Teddy had taken care of them—made sure they were fed and bathed, that Teddy was just as much a victim as they were.

That was why, while Shadow Guardian was fighting the other two, he had snuck back in and stolen a dose of the Build and Burn to give to Teddy. He had only wished he had been able to give him something that would help Teddy find him. They wouldn't tell Joshua anything about him.

Joshua stared out the window of his apartment. *I'll find you. I'll show them what a good guy you are.*

Dion stepped into the office and froze when she saw Juan Carlos on the phone with the poor unfortunate soul that had crossed him. "You tell the mayor that Juan Carlos Sanz is on the phone, and I don't give a damn what he's doing right now. If he's not on this phone in two minutes, we will pull all of our support and put it behind whoever runs against him."

Dion covered her mouth to keep from laughing out loud. Juan Carlos gave her a wink before returning to the conversation on the phone. "Mayor Trainer, this is Juan Carlos, one of your biggest campaign backers, oh, wait, I'm sorry, I *am* your biggest campaign backer. It is so kind of you to finally take my call. I almost had to pull all my fundraising and donations for your next mayoral campaign without giving you the benefit of defending yourself."

This was the Fear of Juan Carlos that so many in the building had heard about, but Dion got to watch it firsthand. "Defend yourself? Well, let's see. Three men wearing bear masks destroyed a city block in North Side, and the police did nothing. Would you care to explain that? What do you mean you know nothing about that? Here, check your email." Juan Carlos hit send on an email he had pending. "That is the estimated damage and pictures of the destroyed city block."

Dion saw Juan Carlos roll his eyes. She knew the weasel was spouting some type of political mumbo jumbo at him. "Let me put it to you this way: Diego and I still have a good number of friends that live there, and we consider that our community. If you can't ensure the security of our community, we're going to back a mayoral candidate that can." Juan Carlos gave Dion a look of disbelief. "You do that and get back to me in forty-eight hours." Juan Carlos paused to let the man speak. "That's nice. I said forty-eight hours."

Juan Carlos hung up the office phone, only to have his cell ring. "Dion, I'm sorry. I have to take this." Juan Carlos put the phone to his ear. "This is Juan Carlos. Oh, my God, that's wonderful news. No, I won't get my hopes up. Thank you for calling. I'll light an extra candle tonight that it all works out for Gato. Goodbye."

Juan Carlos ended the call, only to have the phone ring in his hand. He mouthed *Detective Heath* to her, then answered. "Juan Carlos Sanz, how may I help you? Yes, I'm playing. This Friday? Let me check my schedule."

"You're free!" Dion shouted loud enough to be heard over the phone.

"Apparently, I'm free." Juan Carlos stuck his tongue out at Dion. "Dinner sounds splendid. NO! No, I'll come to you; you don't have to pick me up." Juan Carlos gave Dion an imploring look.

With a sigh, she moved across the room and took the phone from Juan Carlos. "Hello, Detective Heath; this is Dion, Juan Carlos's assistant. The reason you can't pick him up at his place is that you run the risk of running into Diego, and there is a whole set of protocols we have set in place when introducing Diego to a possible significant other. It's for your safety, and it is court-ordered." She handed the phone back to Juan Carlos.

"Why are you laughing? No, she's not joking. Look, I need to get back to work. I'll text you later. Okay. Have a wonderful day at work." Juan Carlos hung the phone up. They both waited for it to ring again before Juan Carlos asked, "Now, what can I do for you?"

He could tell by the way Dion looked at him there was trouble. "They finished the inventory of the warehouse. It wasn't just the Build and Burn chemicals that were taken." She handed her tablet over to Juan Carlos. "Something else was taken."

Juan Carlos read the tablet and gasped. "Oh, dear God."

Shadow Guardian's adventures continue in Shadow Guardian and the Big Bad Wolf.

RECIPE

ONE THING YOU SHOULD KNOW ABOUT ME is that I was the only child of my parents that was born in the United States. My three siblings were all born in Spain, while I was born in Charleston, SC. My father was from Harrisburg, Pennsylvania, and my mother was from Spain. To be exact, she was from Las Cabezas de San Juan, a small town outside of Seville (Sevilla) in Andalucía.

I grew up eating a blend of Spanish and traditional American food. One of the things that I loved to eat was Puchero. It was and is a staple in our home. When I eat Puchero, it's like a warm hug from my mother. You'll notice that I referenced Puchero in the story. Esmerelda made it for Diego and Juan Carlos. She is a Gitana (Gypsy) like me. That means something totally different in Spain than it does in the rest of Europe. You'll learn more in the next Shadow Guardian Book.

Since my mother passed, I've tried to make Puchero, but something was missing. My cousin, Rocio, was kind enough to give me the recipe, and now I'm going to share it with you.

This is traditional cooking without measurements. This recipe is made frequently, mainly because this is a fairly simple recipe that you can make on a hot summer day or a cold winter evening. There are two versions of this recipe, one with rice and one with noodles. First, we'll start with the broth.

What you'll need are garbanzos, a piece of fatback, one whole boiler chicken, salt, carrots, potatoes, and some people put celery in it. If you don't use a whole chicken, you will need some type of chicken bone to help make the broth. You'll need mint for making the noodles or rice. You can substitute the chicken with a turkey leg. Stay tuned at the end of the recipe for a true family story about using turkey for Puchero.

If you're using dried garbanzos, soak them in cold water overnight. If you're using canned garbanzos, you can just pop the can open and use them right away. Get one large pot that will hold the whole chicken. Fill it with water. Add three dashes of salt. You can add more salt to taste. Even if you're using chicken breast and some chicken bones, get a good-sized pot. The broth is key in Puchero.

Add about a handful or so of garbanzos, add about three average-sized potatoes, peeled and cubed, and about six or seven baby carrots. If you're using celery, you'd add about two stems diced, as well. Finally, add the fatback. This is why you don't want to add too much salt at first. The fat back will supply the salt and give it a little flavor.

Now put the pot on medium-high heat, slightly covered, for about two to three hours. You're not going to forget about it. You're going to come back and add water as necessary and scoop out the fat that floats to the top. The broth should take on a cloudy state as it cooks. Once the fatback and the chicken are tender, you can reduce the heat to low. Now, at this point, carefully pull the chicken out of the pot and set it aside to cool off.

From here, you're going to scoop out the broth into another smaller pot to cook your noodles or your rice. Make sure you get some of the vegetables and garbanzos in the broth. Use long grain rice or angel hair pasta for the best results. Add about two springs of mint and bring the broth to a boil. Once boiling, add your rice or noodles. Once they are tender, turn the heat off. I normally do three cups of broth to one cup of rice or a quarter of a box of angel hair pasta, but I'm cooking for one. You want more broth than you do rice or noodles because you're making soup.

Now the chicken should be cool enough to handle. Peel and shred the chicken into a bowl. If you're doing pasta, you can add cubed ham or chop up two boiled eggs per bowl, like I do. Add the rice or noodles from your pot. If you need more juice, pull it from the original pot. Add salt to taste and enjoy!

Now the fatback. Some people will enjoy this as a second course, called la Pringá. The fatback is sliced, put between two pieces of bread, and eaten. Now, this isn't sandwich bread. This would be a good crusty French roll or French bread. I never did that myself, but my mother did.

Okay, so now you have a whole bunch of chicken and a ton of broth. It's not going to waste. Scoop out the broth and divide the chicken up between however many containers you have available and freeze. You can pull it out the night before and put it in a slow cooker to warm up during the day or put it on the stove to heat up over medium heat for about thirty minutes. You may have to add a little water. Then decide if you want rice or noodles.

If you have more chicken than you have broth, throw that bad boy back in the pot and make more Puchero to freeze. If you still have a bunch of chicken left, you can shred the chicken to make croquetas. It's rare I have too much extra chicken because my little diva, Bonita, loves Puchero.

Puchero is really great for when you're not feeling well. Got a cold? Puchero. Upset stomach? Puchero. Broken arm? Puchero when you get back from the doctors. It's a soup, not a miracle cure.

Alright, as promised. The story. This was before I was born. We're talking the early 1970s. My father was stationed in Rota, Spain. Now in Spain, they don't celebrate Thanksgiving. Shocker, right? Well, my dad was craving a traditional Thanksgiving dinner. My mother didn't know how to cook American food, so my father was going to handle everything.

He got everything he needed that week, including a big turkey. Now my abuela (grandmother) was visiting them that week. My father had told my mother not to touch the turkey. He had forgotten to tell my abuela. Can you guess what happened? Well, continue reading anyway.

My mother had left my brothers and sister with my abuela while she went out to run errands. My abuela, wanting to be helpful, decided to make lunch. When she opened the refrigerator, she found my father's turkey. When my mother got home, she didn't think anything about the Puchero my brothers and sister were eating.

When my father got home and was going to get the turkey ready, it was nowhere to be found. He asked my mom where she put the turkey. Of course, my mother had no clue what had happened to the turkey. They began to fight when my grandmother came into the kitchen and asked what they were fighting about.

When my father told her he was looking for the turkey he had in the refrigerator, my abuela went over to the big pot on the stove and told him that she had made Puchero out of it.

She then proceeded to make him a bowl. He ate that Puchero.
He didn't have his traditional Thanksgiving dinner until the
following year. He made sure Abuela wasn't visiting that week.

BOOK CLUB QUESTIONS

1. If Build and Burn were safe and available, would you take it? Why or why not?

2. We find out that Alex has been working at DJC for three years without a raise or promotion. Do you think this is because he didn't like to make waves or he didn't know his value?

3. In order to help Diego succeed, Juan Carlos puts his own life on hold. Would you do that for your child? Why or why not?

4. Jimmy (Teddy) is in love the Timmy (Honey), but Timmy doesn't love him back. Jimmy (Teddy) knows this. Why do you think he does this?

5. This story deals with body image. Even after Jimmy becomes Teddy, he's envious of Honey's and Papa's bodies.

He doesn't seem to be comfortable with his body until Joshua shows interest in him. Do you think Jimmy (Teddy) ties his self-worth to the perception of others?

6. Diego is successful and sexy. He's confident as Shadow Guardian flirting with Alex, but as Diego, he's awkward and goofy. Does the guise of Shadow Guardian give Diego a confidence he does not feel as Diego?

7. Dr. Wyatt convinces Timmy to take Build and Burn so they can "finally be together." If Dr. Wyatt hadn't offered himself as the reward for taking Build and Burn, do you think Timmy would have taken it?

8. Who do you think gave Alex the confidence to call Freddy to go out: Juan Carlos or Shadow Guardian?

9. After Shadow Guardian ends it with Alex, he contemplates going on the apps again. He's deleted them and downloaded them again, only to find men who just want him for sex because men don't date guys like him. Do you think his experiences on the apps affected his perception about himself?

10. When Diego finds out Juan Carlos put a failsafe in his suit, he gets furious at Juan Carlos. Even though it saved his life, he initially wants Juan Carlos to take the failsafe off. Is the failsafe Juan Carlos second guessing Diego or looking out for him? Is Diego justified in initially being angry because of the failsafe?

AUTHOR BIO

ROBERT J. LEWIS IS A GAY WRITER BASED OUT of Charleston, South Carolina. When he's not busy with his plants, being a doggy-daddy, or watching the latest Sci-Fi, he can be found writing. He's influenced by such writers as T.J. Klune, Rhys Ford, Jordan Castillo Price, and L.A. Witt. You can keep up with Robert J. Lewis's latest releases and antics on his social media at <u>Dreams – Robert J. Lewis (robert-j-lewis.com)</u>

MORE BOOKS FROM
4 HORSEMEN PUBLICATIONS

ROMANCE

ANN SHEPPHIRD
The War Council

EMILY BUNNEY
All or Nothing
All the Way
All Night Long: Novella
All She Needs
Having it All
All at Once
All Together
All for Her

KT BOND
Back to Life
Back to Love
Back at Last

MANDY FATE
Love Me, Goaltender
Captain of My Heart

LYNN CHANTALE
The Baker's Touch
Blind Secrets
Broken Lens
Blind Fury
Time Bomb
VIP's Revenge
Chef's Taste

MIMI FRANCIS
Private Lives
Private Protection
Private Party
Run Away Home
The Professor
Our Two-Week, One-Night Stand

SHAE COON
Bound in Love
Controlling Assets
For His Own Protection
Her Broken Pieces
The Roma's Claim
The Roma's Promise

LGBT Romance

Eskay Kabba
Hidden Love
Not So Hidden
Signs of Affection

Lucas LaMont
Roman's Reckoning: Type 6

Mikaél's Moment: Type 6
Stephan's Resurgence: Type 5
Anastasia's Arrival: Type 6

Stormie Skyes
Check Yes, No, or Maybe

Fantasy, SciFi, & Paranormal Romance

Amanda Fasciano
Waking Up Dead
Dead Vessel

Beau Lake
The Beast Beside Me
The Beast Within Me
Taming the Beast: Novella
The Beast After Me
Charming the Beast: Novella
The Beast Like Me
An Eye for Emeralds
Swimming in Sapphires
Pining for Pearls

Chelsea Burton Dunn
By Moonlight

Danielle Orsino
Locked Out of Heaven
Thine Eyes of Mercy
From the Ashes
Kingdom Come
Fire, Ice, Acid, & Heart
A Fae is Done

J.M. Paquette
Klauden's Ring
Solyn's Body
The Inbetween
Hannah's Heart
Call Me Forth
Invite Me In
Keep Me Close

Jessica Salina
Not My Time

Kait Disney-Leugers
Antique Magic

Lyra R. Saenz
Prelude
Falsetto in the Woods: Novella
Ragtime Swing
Sonata
Song of the Sea
The Devil's Trill
Bercuese
To Heal a Songbird
Ghost March
Nocturne

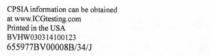

9 798823 200032